Misunderstood

"What are you going to do if that guy you met at the bookstore calls?"

"Who? Oh, you mean Jed." It took a moment before Chloe understood. When she finally realized who Mia was referring to, she had a wonderful idea. "He's not interested in me. Would you like to meet him?"

Mia snorted faintly. "Hey, maybe I'm not as gorgeous as you, but I don't need your castoffs."

Shocked, Chloe gasped. She couldn't believe what her friend had just said. "I didn't mean it like that," she protested. "I just thought you'd like to meet Jed."

"I know what you thought," Mia interrupted. "But I don't need your pity castoffs. I can get my own dates."

Chloe felt like a worm. Why hadn't she kept her mouth shut?

LIFE AT SIXTEEN
Good Intentions

LIFE AT SIXTEEN

Good Intentions

Cheryl Lanham

BERKLEY JAM BOOKS, NEW YORK

GOOD INTENTIONS

A Berkley Jam Book / published by arrangement with
the author

PRINTING HISTORY
Berkley Jam edition / December 1998

All rights reserved.
Copyright © 1998 by Cheryl Arguile.
This book may not be reproduced in whole or in part,
by mimeograph or any other means, without permission.
For information address: The Berkley Publishing Group,
a member of Penguin Putnam Inc.,
375 Hudson Street, New York, New York 10014

The Penguin Putnam Inc. World Wide Web site address is
http://www.penguinputnam.com

ISBN: 0-425-16521-3

BERKLEY JAM BOOKS®
Berkley Jam Books are published by The Berkley Publishing Group,
a member of Penguin Putnam Inc.,
375 Hudson Street, New York, New York 10014.
BERKLEY JAM and its logo are trademarks
belonging to Berkley Publishing Corporation.

PRINTED IN THE UNITED STATES OF AMERICA

10 9 8 7 6 5 4 3 2 1

*This book is dedicated to Robert Domholt,
one of the very best.*

CHAPTER ONE

Landsdale Memorial Hospital really sucked, but it was better than a morgue, Chloe Marlowe thought as she stared at the acoustic ceiling tiles over her bed. Or was it? After what had happened to her, she wasn't sure anymore. She wasn't sure about anything anymore.

She wondered if the whole thing had been a hallucination or if it had been real. She felt funny. Not funny ha-ha—no one, not even her worst enemies, would find what she'd been through amusing—but funny weird. Yeah, she nodded to herself and winced as the movement caused her head to ache, she felt real weird. Like she wasn't herself anymore. Almost as if she was someone else wearing Chloe's skin. But she could remember everything. She knew her name, where she lived, who her friends were (not that she had all that many), who her enemies were (lots of those), and what she looked like.

"Wow," she muttered, "what if I look in a mirror and it's not me anymore?" She hadn't bothered to ask to see a mirror. Since she'd regained consciousness last night, she really hadn't cared what she'd looked like. That thought alone should have tipped her off that something really bizarre had happened. The old Chloe would have demanded a mirror within ten seconds of opening her eyes. Old Chloe? What the heck did that mean? She was still her.

Maybe that was the problem.

She wasn't sure she wanted to be. Chloe Marlowe wasn't a very nice person. She knew that now.

Chloe shook herself and gingerly pulled up to a sitting position. For a moment, the room spun as she fought off a wave of nausea. Then the television and two chairs at the foot of her bed stopped tap-dancing and she felt like she could risk moving without keeling over.

She swung her legs over the side of the bed, took a deep breath, and pushed herself onto her feet. She stood still for a few seconds to make sure she wouldn't get dizzy and then slowly shuffled toward the sink. Right above it was a mirror.

As she got closer, she reached out and grabbed the side of the sink for support. She kept her eyes on her feet, telling herself it was because she wanted to make sure she didn't trip.

Once she was safely propped against the edge of the porcelain, she looked up. Still Chloe Marlowe. Of course, her normally clear green eyes were now shadowed by dark circles, her sun-streaked dark blonde hair, for which she paid a fortune for the natural look, was now lank and hanging limply around her face;

her smooth, tanned skin was pasty looking and pale. But under the grunge, it was still her.

Chloe went absolutely still as an unfamiliar emotion swept across her in a heated rush. It took her a moment to identify exactly what she was feeling.

Disappointment.

Good grief. She shook her head in confusion, this time ignoring the searing pain that shot up from the side of her neck to the top of her skull. Why should she be disappointed? Considering she'd almost been killed, she ought to be grateful.

She didn't understand. Her heart had stopped for a full three minutes. She'd died. She ought to be glad she was back with the living.

Maybe that was the problem. She was delighted to be alive. She was disappointed she was still Chloe.

"Oh, for crying out loud," she muttered, turning away from the image in the mirror. "Who else would you be?"

Anyone would be better than who she was. She stopped as that thought came into her mind. Chloe stood stock-still for a moment before she shuffled back across the short space and flopped onto her bed. Something was happening to her. Something she didn't like but didn't seem to have any control over.

Panicked, she forced another slow, deep breath into her lungs. There was obviously a reasonable explanation for all these strange feelings. It must be all the drugs and stuff they'd given her to start her heart up, or maybe it was that electric chest-thumping thing.

Yeah, that had to be it, she told herself. She'd be her old self again in a day or two. These weirdo feelings would go away and she could get back to her normal life. Speaking of which, why wasn't someone with her? Didn't they usually have people hanging around when someone woke up from a coma? Where were her people? Where was Dad or Lucinda? For that matter, where was the nurse? Wasn't there always a nurse in intensive care?

Chloe looked around her room and realized she wasn't in intensive care. She was in a normal hospital room. They must have moved her last night, she thought. Maybe they needed her space. But she was sure she'd been in intensive care, because on the way here in the ambulance, she'd heard them on the radio talking about her. She frowned as she realized she couldn't remember exactly what had happened. An accident? Sure. That was it. Besides, she could sort of remember intensive care and a . . . She was going to drive herself nuts, she decided. The only thing that was really clear in her mind was the one thing she refused to think about. It was too weird, too scary. For the rest, she'd just wait and talk to her dad or Lucinda when they finally got here. But she was a little hurt all the same. You'd think someone would be here. After all, her heart had stopped. She'd *died*, for Pete's sake.

"Oh good, you're awake again." A nurse walked in unannounced. "Do you need any help going to the bathroom? I know you went on your own earlier this morning, but lots of patients force themselves up just so they can get the IV out. Don't be shy about asking if you need help."

"I don't need to go," Chloe replied. "You were in

here earlier? When?'' She couldn't remember the plump, dark-haired woman.

''When I first came on shift.'' She straightened Chloe's pillows and pulled the wrinkles out of her bottom sheet. ''Don't you remember? It was a little past midnight. You proved you could go to the bathroom on your own so I took your IV out.'' She smiled sympathetically. ''Having trouble remembering? Don't worry, that's normal. You took quite a whack on your head, but you're going to be just fine.''

''Oh good, you're out of bed.'' Lucinda Marlowe, Chloe's stepmother, smiled carefully from the doorframe. ''You look like you're doing well.''

She wasn't. She was so confused her head was spinning, but for some reason she couldn't understand, she decided not to ask any more questions.

''I'm feeling a lot better,'' Chloe said, returning her stepmother's smile with one of her own. ''Come on in, I could use a visitor.''

Lucinda drew back in surprise. ''Even me?''

''I'll be back with your breakfast in a few minutes,'' the nurse promised, nodding at Lucinda as she passed.

Chloe stared at her stepmother. She wondered why she didn't feel the flush of anger her beautiful stepmother's appearance usually triggered. But she didn't. As a matter of fact, a vague sense of something else was creeping into the back of her mind. She wasn't sure she knew what it was, but it was there all right. The undefined feeling made her want to hide, to put her head under the sheet and not face the world, especially not her stepmother. But instead of acting on the oddball emotion, Chloe kept her bright smile on and said, "Especially you. Come on in, really. I'm glad you're here."

Lucinda Marlowe was in her late forties but had the kind of superb skin and bone structure which took ten years off her age. With her dark brown hair swirling around her shoulders and her tall, slim figure, she could still turn heads when she walked into a room. Her sapphire blue eyes narrowed in suspicion. "All right. Your father'll be here in a few minutes—he's still parking the car."

Chloe didn't blame Lucinda for being wary—she'd not given the woman much reason to like her since she'd married Dan Marlowe, Chloe's father, almost a year ago. "Good, we'll have a few minutes together before he comes."

Lucinda's mouth flattened into a thin, hard line. "Look, Chloe, if you're going to go on about that money—"

"No, no"—Chloe quickly raised her hand—"that's not it at all. As a matter of fact, I'm really sorry about what happened. . . ." Her voice trailed off as she suddenly realized what the strange, unknown emotion was: shame. She was ashamed of the way she'd behaved. Truly, deeply, and sincerely ashamed. Now where on earth was that coming from?

"You?" Lucinda interrupted. "Sorry? Come on now, this is me you're talking to, remember? You might have come close to dying, dear, but unless they gave you a personality transplant in that emergency room, I know damned good and well you're not sorry about anything except that your little scheme didn't work.''

"No, really. . . ." She broke off as she heard the familiar slap of her father's sandals against the linoleum floor outside in the hall. "Hi, Dad." She summoned another bright smile as Dan Marlowe came into the room.

"Hi, honey," he said, returning her smile. He was a tall man with curly black hair liberally sprinkled with gray. His face, deeply tanned from playing golf and sailing, was creased in worry as he studied his daughter. "How are you feeling?"

"I'm fine," Chloe said. Something was seriously off. She ought to hate Lucinda—she had hated Lucinda for almost a year now. But she didn't. Instead, looking at her dad, she felt a swell of affection and gratitude that he had someone he loved who loved him. "When did I come here?"

Her father's worried frown intensified. "Oh my God," Dan said. "You mean you don't remember? Good Lord, the doctor's doing up your discharge papers now. Maybe I'd better stop him. Maybe they ought to keep you a little longer, make sure there aren't any aftereffects from the accident."

Lucinda, who'd stepped back from the bed, crossed her arms over her chest and looked disgusted. Chloe wanted to scream with frustration. Her stepmother's body language clearly said she thought Chloe was faking it. Chloe could hardly blame her. It wouldn't be the first time she'd pretended to be sick to get her own way.

"There aren't any aftereffects; I'm fine," she said,

just as Dan's hand reached for the nurse's buzzer. "Don't call anyone. I'm just a little confused as to what time I got here, that's all I meant."

Lucinda's expression turned wary again.

"Thank God." Dan slumped in relief and drew back from the bed. "Don't scare your old man that way, honey. The accident was bad enough."

"I'm fine, really. I guess I'm just a little fuzzy about the sequence of events. But that's okay, I remember now." She had to get out of here. She had to find someone she could talk to, someone she could trust. Something was wrong. Something was causing her to feel things she shouldn't and to act funny. And it wasn't just because she'd wrapped her Beamer around a tree and cracked her head hard.

Maybe that whole scene in the ambulance hadn't been a hallucination. Maybe it had been for real.

"Perhaps we ought to let Chloe get ready to go." Lucinda took Dan's arm. "She still has to eat breakfast and get dressed before she's discharged."

"Thanks, Lucinda," Chloe said sincerely. She cringed inwardly as she saw the look of surprise flash across her father's face. Good grief, had she been such a witch that even a few polite words could cause people to be so darned shocked? Apparently so. "It's going to take me a while to get dressed—I move pretty slow. Did you happen to bring me any clothes?"

"We brought them last night when they moved you out of intensive care." Dan jerked his chin toward the closet next to the sink. Then he reached over and stroked her hand. "We'll be back in an hour or so, okay?"

"Okay. I'll see you later." Chloe sank back against the pillows as they left. God, she had to make sense of this. She flashed back to the ambulance, trying to force herself to remember.

Suddenly, the fuzziness was gone and everything came back to her. Everything. The way the young paramedic's hands had been everywhere at once, easing the oxygen mask over her mouth, whipping out that little flashlight pencil to look into her eyes, then finally getting out that shocking electronic box and zapping her chest. Weird, she hadn't felt a thing when they'd done that, and she knew she should have.

She had to talk to someone. But she knew that neither her father nor her stepmother would understand.

Chloe had to find someone.

Someone who would listen to her and not tell her she was as nutty as the top of a hot fudge sundae. Somebody who would help her understand what was happening to her.

The trouble was, she didn't have anyone remotely like that.

Chloe Marlowe wasn't exactly the most popular girl in town.

"How are you feeling?" Dr. Steadman, young, dark haired and handsome in a nerdy kind of way, stood by her bedside reading her latest vitals off the chart.

"Pretty good," Chloe replied. Normally, she'd be mortified at looking so hideous in front of a nice-looking guy, but right now she was more concerned with getting answers to her questions than with the fact that it was a bad-hair day. "But I'm a little confused."

"That's normal," he said, making a note on the chart. "You got quite a crack on your skull."

"Is that all that's wrong with me?" Chloe hadn't sat through years of soap operas and doctor shows for nothing. By listening carefully and taking a quick peek at her chart, she'd worked out that she'd been admitted into the emergency room two nights ago with a head injury. Someone had noted on the chart that she'd been resuscitated in the ambulance.

He looked up from the chart and stared at her over the rims of his way-cool glasses. "Isn't that enough?"

"Oh that's plenty," she replied. "But I want to know if I only had a concussion, why was I resuscitated in the ambulance?"

He frowned disapprovingly and then walked over and put the chart back in the little bin on the wall next to the door. He was stalling.

Chloe knew that tactic. She'd used it lots of times herself. Generally when one of her schemes had blown up in her face and her father was calling her on the carpet for it. She mentally cringed again as the memory of some of the things she'd done came back with a vengeance. Then she brushed them aside. Right now she needed answers. She would have plenty of time to atone for her past later. "Doctor?" she prompted.

"Have you discussed this with your father?" He kept his back to her.

"No, why should I?" she asked. "I know I was

resuscitated—I've got the spot on my chest to prove it. I want to know why.''

''According to the paramedics''—the doctor turned to face her—''you were breathing fine when they pulled you out of the car. But for some reason, in the ambulance, your heart stopped.''

''Any idea why?''

He clasped his hands together and shrugged. ''Look, I don't want to talk about it.''

''Why?'' Chloe sighed in disgust. ''Oh, for goodness' sake, I'm not going to sue you. It wasn't the paramedic's fault that my heart stopped.''

''Try telling your father that,'' he burst out. ''Look, we're not supposed to discuss the circumstances or the ambulance ride. Your father's the most prominent lawyer in Landsdale. He was upset enough when he found out about the accident, but when he learned that you had to be resuscitated in the ambulance he really came unglued. He decided the paramedics must have done something wrong and now he's threatening to sue everyone.''

''He won't,'' Chloe said firmly. She wouldn't let him. To stop him, however, she'd need some answers. ''But I've got to know what happened if I'm going to stop him from filing suit.''

''That's just it,'' Dr. Steadman replied. ''No one knows what happened. One minute your vital signs were just fine and then thirty seconds later, your breathing and your heart had stopped.''

''Had the paramedics given me any drugs?'' she asked. ''Maybe I'm allergic to something they gave me.''

"They hadn't given you anything. They were really careful, too—that car of yours was totaled, but you got lucky and they were able to pull you out without any trouble at all. You were fuzzy but your heartbeat was strong, your blood pressure good, and you were breathing okay. There weren't any injuries that anyone could see so they put you in the ambulance and started in. Jon Barton—that's the paramedic—said that it just looked like you had a bad bump on your head. You even talked to them a little bit when they first got there."

"Then what happened?"

"Nothing." Dr. Steadman shook his head. "And that's the mystery. They followed standard operating procedure and hooked you up to a monitor for the ride in. It's a good thing they did, too, because all of a sudden the monitor started beeping like mad. You had no heartbeat, no respiratory rate, and no brain activity. That's when they resuscitated you."

"How long was I, uh . . ." She wasn't sure how to ask this question. "Out?"

"Three minutes."

"That means for three minutes nothing registered on the monitor in the ambulance?"

"Right. That's what's so disturbing. There's nothing wrong with you but a mild concussion. No internal injuries, no allergies, and no drugs or alcohol in your system. Nothing. Yet for three minutes, you were . . ." He broke off, hesitant to use the word in front of the daughter of the man who was one of the best lawyers in California.

"Dead," she finished. "Don't worry, you don't

have to be afraid I'll use this conversation against you. I'll make sure my dad doesn't sue anyone." She would, too; she didn't know how, but she knew that what had happened to her in that ambulance wasn't due to a paramedic's doing something wrong or causing her to fall into a coma because she was allergic to something they'd given her. She didn't know how she was certain, but she was.

"I'm not sure you'll be able to stop him," Dr. Steadman replied. "He was pretty upset and frankly, I don't blame him. After they resuscitated you, you went into a coma. You spent over twenty-four hours in intensive care. You were hooked up to every expensive piece of monitoring equipment we have, and the only thing that's wrong with you is a mild concussion. It's a mystery, Chloe—I don't mind admitting that."

"You mean I just snapped out of it?" Chloe could vaguely remember opening her eyes and seeing worried faces hovering all around her.

"That's right. Last night, you suddenly woke up and said you were hungry." He grinned. "Everyone was very relieved."

"Yeah," she muttered, "I'll bet they were. So let me see if I understand this: I've been in a coma but now I'm fine. Right?"

"Right," he agreed. "It's why you went into a coma that puzzles us. That, and why you had to be resuscitated in the first place. There's no medical reason for what happened to you. We've done dozens of tests in the past forty-eight hours and frankly, we're no closer to finding an answer. You simply stopped breathing.''

''But only for three minutes,'' she said. ''I was only dead for a few minutes, right?''

''Lucinda wanted to come,'' her father said as he helped her out of the wheelchair and into the front seat of his Cadillac, ''but I told her to stay home and get things ready. I want my little girl to enjoy her welcome-home dinner.''

Her father was lying, but Chloe smiled politely anyway. She understood perfectly. Now that her stepdaughter wasn't facing the grim reaper, Lucinda wanted to stay as far away from her as possible. Chloe didn't blame her. She'd acted like a real witch to her stepmother. But that was all going to end.

She wasn't confused anymore. Chloe knew exactly what she had to do.

She stared out the car window, watching as her father pushed the wheelchair over to the waiting orderly. Dan Marlowe flashed his famous smile and reached for his wallet. ''Let me give you a little something for your trouble.''

''That's not necessary, Mr. Marlowe.'' The young man, who wasn't more than a couple of years older than Chloe, raised his hands in a gesture of protest and shook his head. ''It was no trouble. I'm a volunteer. I like helping take care of people.''

Chloe closed her eyes as envy rippled through her. He *liked* taking care of others; he liked helping. One part of her sort of understood what he was talking about while another part of her didn't because, if the truth were known, she'd never helped take care of anyone but herself her entire life.

"Nice kid," her father muttered when he got in the car. "They probably told him to be real nice. They're scared of a lawsuit."

"He's not scared of a lawsuit," she heard herself say. "He's a genuinely good person, can't you tell? There's an aura around him. . . ." She clamped her mouth shut as she heard the words leave her mouth. What was wrong with her? Was she nuts? She blinked and looked straight ahead. "I mean, he seemed like a nice person, that's all."

"Sorry, honey." He chuckled and turned on the ignition. "I didn't mean to sound so cynical. Of course he's not scared of a lawsuit, he's only a volunteer."

"You're not going to sue," she said flatly.

"I've got my people working on it," he replied, looking back as he cautiously pulled out of the parking space. "They screwed up big time, sweetie. Those damned paramedics almost killed you. They did something to you that made your heart stop. It's a miracle you didn't die."

It was a miracle all right, but not the kind her father thought. "It wasn't their fault," she argued. "They didn't do anything to me."

He turned out of the parking lot and onto Larchmont Boulevard, the huge main thoroughfare that bisected the town of Landsdale. "Honey, all you've got is a mild concussion. Yet you spent over twenty-four hours in intensive care. Something's wrong. That shouldn't have happened."

Chloe sighed and turned her attention back to the window. They sped through Landsdale quickly, past the brand-new shopping mall and into the newer part of town, to the expensive housing tracts on the west side. They lived in the most exclusive tract of all—the most expensive house, too.

"Sometimes, you know," she murmured, "things do happen and it's nobody's fault."

"Nonsense," her father replied cheerfully. "It's always somebody's fault."

"Dad, they didn't do anything," she insisted. "Besides, why do you want to sue? I'm okay."

"But what if you hadn't been?" he shot back. His face was grim and his eyes worried.

She realized that his threats weren't just because he was a hotshot lawyer who always liked to win. He'd been genuinely scared she'd die. That made her feel a little better.

But she still had to talk him out of this lawsuit. What had happened to her hadn't been the result of any human action. He'd never believe that, though. She wasn't sure she'd believe it herself if the situation were reversed.

"But I am just fine," she said earnestly. "And I think that instead of running around threatening to sue, you ought to be saying a prayer of thanksgiving. I mean, the paramedics didn't do anything wrong. They followed standard operating procedure."

He looked at her sharply, his expression troubled. Then he quickly turned his attention back to the road. "You don't know what you're saying. You were unconscious—you can't know what they did."

But she did know. She could describe it in detail. If she had to, she'd do it from a witness stand.

"You've had a nasty shock," he concluded.

She'd had a lot more than a nasty shock, but there wouldn't be any point in trying to tell him that. She'd have to show him. She'd have to show all of them.

"I'm fine, Dad," she said wearily. "Please, let's talk about the lawsuit later. I just want to enjoy the sunshine and the pretty day and enjoy being here in one piece to experience it all."

"All right, honey," he agreed.

But she saw the puzzled expression flash across his face and she would have laughed except that she was afraid if she started, she wouldn't be able to stop. The only time she'd ever noticed the weather before had been to complain if it was raining. "I'm looking forward to being home. Hospitals aren't exactly fun places."

"We're looking forward to having you home," he assured her. He reached over and patted her arm as they turned onto Seward Drive, the most exclusive cul-de-sac in the entire tract. Chloe had once felt such pride when they made this drive up the hill. The houses were all huge Spanish-style five- and six-bedroom numbers. The smallest lot size was a quarter acre and the views of the Pacific Ocean in one direction and the mountains in the other were spectacular. Now, all she felt was a disorienting sense of displacement, as though she didn't belong here at all.

He pulled into the driveway of their home, a six-bedroom mansion enclosed in a beautiful courtyard and with a balcony off most of the bedrooms. There was a lush backyard behind the house, a pool and Jacuzzi, too.

"We're going to have a nice, quiet celebration now that you're all right. Then we'll tuck you in upstairs and you can recuperate to your heart's content," her father said. He opened the door and climbed out.

Chloe opened her own door and got out.

"You need some help, honey?" her father asked.

"I'm fine," she replied. "Who all is going to be here tonight?" She wondered who they could have found to celebrate with her. The only friend she had was Mia.

"Just family. You, me, and Lucinda." He started for the courtyard. "Oh yeah, and Nick will be joining us too. I thought you'd like having at least one young person there."

"Nick's going to be here? I thought he was staying at his uncle Bobby's until school started."

"Lucinda asked him to come home." Her father held open the gate for her. "He's family now. You don't mind, do you?"

"Of course not," she said, again seeing the surprise flash across his face. "As you said, he's family now."

Nick Mallory was Lucinda's son.

He hated Chloe's guts.

"I'm sure it'll be a fun evening," she said. "Real fun."

CHAPTER
TWO

Chloe stepped through the six-foot-tall gate and into the courtyard. She moved to one side so her father could pass and then hesitated, seeing the familiar surroundings out of new eyes.

The courtyard was beautiful. Overhead, a latticework of wooden crossbeams was covered with a deep layer of crisp, green ivy sheltering the place from the hot August sun. Wooden planters filled with fuchsias and geraniums hung from the rafters. The floor was paved with deep red Spanish tiles and along the sides of the high fence there were tubs of brightly colored peonies and poppies. In the center of the courtyard was a fountain with a statue of a cherub pouring water out of a bucket into a big base. The soothing tinkling of the water gave the place a peaceful, almost spiritual air. Chloe wondered why she'd never noticed it before.

Then again, she thought as she hurried to catch up with her father, there were a lot of things she'd never noticed.

"We're back," Dan called as they went into the foyer.

"In here," Lucinda's voice came from the living room.

Dan took Chloe's arm and led her across the polished oak floor of the hallway to a short set of steps which went down to the sunken living room. "Careful of the step, honey," he warned.

Her feet sank into the thick, gray carpet. Over her head, a cathedral ceiling soared a good twenty feet, the perfect setting for the elegant silver chandelier that hung over the center of the room. The walls were a pale, cool gray, tastefully decorated with prints and original abstract paintings. Opposite the stairs was a large marble fireplace on top of which stood several pieces of modern crystal. Chloe had never realized how cold the room was. Even the rich, jewel colors of the furniture didn't warm the place up much.

"Hello, Chloe," Lucinda said. She was sitting at one end of the long, green and pink paisley sofa. In her hand, she held a drink. She took a sip. "How are you feeling?"

Guilty and miserable, Chloe thought, but she didn't say it. "I'm fine," she murmured. "Really good."

"Go sit down, honey," Dan said, urging her toward the bright, emerald green overstuffed chair sitting catty-corner to the sofa. "You don't want to tire yourself out."

"I can move around, Dad," she said. "The doctor said I was supposed to be fairly active. Where's Carlotta?"

"She's mixing up a batch of lemonade, from

scratch. That's the only kind you like, isn't it?" Lucinda replied.

"She shouldn't go to any trouble," she muttered. Chloe had a strong urge to go and greet the maid. She didn't know why. Carlotta didn't like her either. "But if she's doing all that just for me, I'll go and help."

This time she didn't see the puzzled frowns her father and his wife exchanged.

Chloe hurried into the kitchen. Like the other rooms in the house, the kitchen was beautifully decorated. Again, like the rest of the house, it was as cold as an ice crystal. The floor was black Italian tile, the appliances chic stainless steel, and the light fixtures so high-tech you'd think you were in the galley of the starship *Enterprise*.

Carlotta Dunkirk was standing at the center island. A pitcher filled with icy lemonade, half a dozen used lemon halves, and a crock of sugar were on the counter in front of her. She turned as she heard Chloe's approach. "Well, so they let you out of the hospital." She was a small, thin woman of sixty with short, gray hair and horn-rimmed glasses. She wore a gray maid's dress and sensible white shoes with thick soles that moved soundlessly through the house. She'd snuck up on Chloe more than once in those shoes.

"Yeah, they did." Chloe was suddenly shy. That in and of itself was unsettling. Carlotta had been with them since Chloe's mom died seven years ago. Chloe hadn't been very nice to Carlotta. In fact, she'd done some really crappy things. The only reason Carlotta

had stayed was because Dan Marlowe paid her
enough to make it worth her while to put up with a
spoiled seventeen-year-old brat.

Chloe didn't understand what was driving her, she
only knew she had to make things right. She wasn't
sure how much time she had. She frowned. Where
had that come from?

"Your lemonade's almost ready. I'm just giving it
a minute for the ice to chill some." Carlotta turned
back to her task and began tossing lemon halves into
the built-in garbage receptacle on the top of the island.

"I'm not in any hurry. You shouldn't have gone to
so much trouble."

Carlotta snorted faintly but didn't turn around.

Chloe swallowed nervously. How should she do
this? Should she just blurt out that she was sorry she'd
been such a pain in the ass? Yeah. That was it. A
straight-out frontal assault. There wasn't any reason
to beat around the bush here. "Carlotta, I'm really
sorry."

Carlotta turned, her expression clearly surprised.
"Sorry? About what?"

"About everything, about acting so obnoxious,"
Chloe said quickly, for some reason wanting to get
the words out as fast as possible. "I haven't been very
nice to you and you've been real good to me. I never
appreciated you and I did things which were pretty
crappy. I'm sorry."

Carlotta's expression changed. Her mouth flattened
to a thin, disapproving line and her eyes narrowed in
suspicion. "You're apologizin' to me?"

"I've been a real creep. I'm really sorry." Chloe

walked over and stopped in front of her. "Honestly, I'd give anything to take back some of the crummy things I've done to you."

Carlotta hesitated, then shrugged and turned her back. "All right. You're sorry." She lifted the tray. "Now, I'd better get this lemonade out there. I don't want your dad to get upset at me."

"Can I help?" Chloe asked. She could tell that Carlotta was barely humoring her. She didn't believe her. Didn't believe her at all. But then, why should she?

"I can manage," Carlotta called as she pushed through the door to the hall.

Chloe closed her eyes and slumped against the counter. This wasn't going well at all. If Carlotta didn't believe she was sincere, no one else would. She'd done some lousy things to the housekeeper, but she'd done worse things to others.

"Nice try, Chloe. What are you going for now? Sympathy or support? Oh, that's right, you're going to need a few friends now that you've totaled your wheels."

Chloe whirled around. Nick Mallory, a bag of chips in his hand, leaned against the door of the walk-in pantry.

He was a tall, dark-haired nineteen year old. His eyes were brown, his features perfect, and his skin tanned from weekends working on his uncle's ranch. He stared at her, an expression of contempt on his face.

"Eavesdropping, Nick?" she asked.

"Not deliberately," he replied. "I, unlike some

people around here, have a few principles.''

''If you've got so many principles you might have let me know you were in there,'' she shot back. ''And for your information, that apology was sincere. I wasn't trying to con her into letting me use her car.''

''Sure you were sincere.'' He tossed the chips down and leaned against the counter. ''Just like you were sincere when you went running to your father with that big lie about my mom.''

She cringed. ''Look, I was wrong about that. But I've been wrong about a lot of things. I'm going to try and make up for it now. I've got a second chance, and I want to make up for all the bad things I've done.''

Nick pushed away from the counter and folded his arms over his chest. He stared at her intently, his gaze focusing hard on her eyes. ''Are you on something?''

''Only aspirin,'' she said excitedly. She still wasn't sure what had happened to her, but now she thought she might have found someone to help her sort it out. Nick was a philosophy major at the University of California at Santa Barbara. He, at least, might listen to her with an open mind.

''Are you sure?''

''Yes. I've got a mild concussion—they don't give you anything for that except a few over-the-counter pills. But look, now that you're here, you've got to help me with something. . . .''

''After that number you pulled on my mom I wouldn't help you cross the street if you were blind,'' he snapped. ''I don't know who the hell you think you are, Chloe, but a few kind words after you've had a scare and faced the grim reaper aren't going to make up for all the misery you've caused."

"I know," she tried again. "I'm really, really sorry. I'll do whatever I can to make it up—"

"There's nothing you can do," he interrupted, backing away from her as though she were contaminated. "You accused my mother of stealing from your father and then you dummied up some phony evidence to prove your point. Good God, girl, you're a monster. Just look at all the crap you've pulled, all the people you've alienated. You know, for someone who's supposed to be Landsdale High's most popular girl, the only person who showed up at the hospital when you were in intensive care was Mia. And I don't know why she bothered, considering that you treat her like dirt."

"People can change," Chloe cried. "The accident changed me. . . ."

"Get real," he scoffed. "You've been watching too much TV. No one changes that fast."

"But they do," she pleaded. "I did. You've got to believe me. I am so sorry. . . ."

"Forget it. You can't waltz in here and say you're sorry and think everything's going to be hunky-dory."

"I know it's not going to be easy—" she began.

"Easy?" He laughed. "Get a grip, Chloe. It's going to be impossible."

He turned on his heel and walked out.

Chloe stared at the bag of chips he'd left on the counter. Her spirits plummeted. Unfortunately, she had the feeling that her stepbrother was right: No one was going to believe she was sincere. Even if she could convince people she was sorry, that still wouldn't make up for some of the awful things she'd done.

The list was fairly long.

And ugly.

She'd made Carlotta's life miserable, that was for sure. She'd whined about the food the woman cooked, never lifted a finger to help with the housework, and worst of all, talked her father into denying Carlotta's request for weekends off. She hadn't wanted to be inconvenienced with having to fend for herself, so when Carlotta had asked for her two days off together, she'd thrown such a fit her father had said no.

Chloe felt like pond scum. Carlotta had wanted those days off so she could spend her weekends with her sister in San Diego. A sister who had Parkinson's disease. She couldn't believe she'd been so selfish. Thank goodness Lucinda had intervened. At least Carlotta had gotten every other weekend off. Chloe added that to her mental list of things she had to do: make sure Carlotta got every weekend off. They were all adults—well, sort of, she thought. They could fend for themselves.

And then there was Lucinda. Chloe started for the living room. She'd have to make sure she did something about her. She owed the poor woman a lot more than an apology.

She'd spent the last year trying to break up her marriage.

Chloe wondered how on earth she could atone for that.

• • •

"I had Carlotta fix your favorite," her father enthused as he helped himself to a large spoonful of chicken fajitas from the sizzling platter in the center of the table. "You need to keep up your strength, doesn't she, Lucinda?"

"Yes," Lucinda replied. She glanced across at Nick, who was sitting next to Chloe, and smiled wanly.

"Go on," her father urged Chloe, "help yourself. Take plenty—you're too thin anyway."

A deep sense of shame swept over her. Despite her father's efforts, dinner was the pits. Lucinda barely spoke, Nick kept his attention on his plate, and even Carlotta moved as fast as she could to get out of the tense, uptight atmosphere. Chloe didn't blame her— she didn't want to be here either. Trouble was, she had nowhere else to go. She was so confused she couldn't think straight, and she was fast getting sick of the idea that she'd been such a horrible person.

She smiled at her father and spooned the spicy chicken mixture onto the flour tortilla on her plate. "Thanks," she murmured, putting the utensil back on the platter. "Would you care for some?" she asked Nick as she moved the heavy plate toward him.

His eyebrows rose slightly and her spirits sank even lower (if that was possible). Was she so terrible that people were surprised when she was just polite? The truth, awful as it was, was yes.

Chloe wished she could crawl into bed and pull the covers over her head. She couldn't think about what had happened to her, she couldn't understand anything, she could only act. Follow her instincts. Try to atone. "Atone" . . . she really liked that word. It seemed to convey exactly what she felt.

She cleared her throat. "Uh, if it's okay with everyone I'd like to say something."

Her father looked at her in surprise, Lucinda regarded her skeptically, and beside her she heard a faint snort of derision from Nick.

"Okay, sweetie," her father said. "Go ahead."

"I know you're all going to find this hard to believe," she began, "but as God is my witness, it's true."

"Oh." Her father smiled widely and put his fork down. "This does sound serious. You've got everyone's attention now."

Carlotta, a pitcher of margaritas in her hand, came into the dining room and placed the container next to him.

"I'd like Carlotta to hear this too," Chloe said.

"Hear what?" Carlotta groused. "I've got to brew the coffee. . . ."

"This will only take a minute," Chloe promised, "and I'll be happy to brew the coffee. You're a member of the household and this involves you, so I think you'd better listen."

"You don't know how to make coffee," Lucinda murmured. But her expression had changed a little, and she looked slightly less skeptical.

"Then it's about time I learned," Chloe said firmly. "I'm seventeen—it wouldn't hurt for me to help out a little around here. But that's not what I wanted to talk about." She waited a moment while

Carlotta sat down at the empty place next to Lucinda.

"All right, honey." Dan nodded encouragingly. "Go ahead, talk."

As she gazed at the faces staring at her expectantly, she realized that what she was going to say would sound crazy. She made a quick decision. She'd confess and apologize first, then she'd tell them the rest. If they didn't believe her, at least she'd have tried.

"First of all, I'd like to apologize to everyone," she said. "I know I've been a pretty lousy person, but I promise, I'm really going to try hard to make it up to everyone."

No one reacted except her father. He reached over and patted her on the hand. "Now, now, sweetheart, don't get all maudlin on us. You don't have anything to apologize for."

Chloe shook her head vehemently. Dear old Dad was part of the problem. She didn't know why she hadn't seen that before. She wasn't trying to lay the blame on him—she was quite willing to take responsibility for herself—but one of the reasons she was such a spoiled brat was because ever since her mother had died, he'd indulged her every whim. Why had it taken her so long to understand that? "Yes I do," she said. "I've been a terrible person. A spoiled brat."

"No you haven't, honey." Dan leaned toward her. "You're overwrought. Take it easy. You've had a tough time."

"No I haven't," she argued, "I've been a self-centered cow. But that's all going to change."

From the corner of her eye, she could see that she had Nick's full, if skeptical, attention. Across the table, Lucinda was also staring at her warily.

"For starters, I'd like to apologize to Carlotta."
She plunged onward as she heard the housekeeper's
gasp of shock. "I was a real witch when she asked to
have weekends off."

"I can make do with what I've got," Carlotta said
quickly. "Every other weekend is fine."

"No it's not," Chloe persisted. She turned and
looked at the housekeeper. "Your sister has a terrible
illness and you should spend your time with her. She
needs you. We're all adults—we ought to be able to
fend for ourselves."

"But I don't need to go every weekend," Carlotta
protested.

"What are you trying to do?" Nick hissed in
Chloe's ear. "Get her fired? Carlotta needs this job."

"No one said anything about Carlotta losing her
job," Chloe objected. Jeez, people automatically
thought the worst of her. "I just want to make it clear
that if Dad can give her weekends off to be with her
sister, I'll take up the slack while she's gone."

"*You'll* take up the slack?" Lucinda said incredulously.

"Yes, me," Chloe shot back. "I know I can't do
much, but I'm not a complete idiot. I can read a cook-
book and do some basic cooking and cleaning. The
important thing is that Carlotta needs to be with her
sister." She looked at her father. He looked slightly
amused. It was the same expression he always had
when he was indulging one of her whims. Like when
she'd taken up horseback riding or surfing.

"It's all right with me," he finally said, "but I will

expect you to hold up your end of the bargain. I can't boil water and I do get hungry. You'll cook, okay?''

"Okay." Chloe smiled happily and glanced at the housekeeper. "Is it all right with you?"

Carlotta got to her feet and shrugged. "It's fine with me. But just remember, Mr. Marlowe, we can always change it back if things don't work out."

As soon as the housekeeper disappeared into the kitchen, Chloe looked at Lucinda. "I'd like to apologize to you, too. I did a terrible, terrible thing."

Lucinda said nothing, merely stared at her.

"You were a little jealous, Chloe," her father said quickly, "that's all. But all's well that ends well. . . ."

"All isn't well," Chloe said fiercely, "and we can't gloss over the way I behaved with saying I was a little jealous. I was a monster to Lucinda. For goodness' sake, Dad. I tried to make you believe she'd stolen from you. I lied and I dummied up false evidence. . . ."

"That doesn't matter anymore," Lucinda said. "And don't waste your breath apologizing, Chloe. You've achieved your goal."

Panic gripped her. "What goal?"

It was Nick who answered. "Don't pretend you don't know. You can cut the act now. You're getting what you want."

"This isn't an act," Chloe cried. "What's going on?"

"We weren't going to say anything until you were feeling stronger," her father said, "but as you don't seem to be suffering any ill effects from the accident, I guess there's no reason not to get it out in the open.

Lucinda and I have decided to go our separate ways. We're getting a divorce.''

"A divorce!" Chloe wailed. "Oh no, you can't."

Lucinda threw her napkin down and shoved back from the table. "I think I'll go upstairs now—I've got a lot of packing to do."

"I'm not hungry, either." Nick, with a disgusted glance at Chloe, followed his mother out of the dining room.

"This is all wrong." Chloe turned to her father. "You're making a mistake, Dad. You love Lucinda and she loves you. If I hadn't spent the last year interfering in your marriage . . ."

"Our decision has nothing to do with you." He reached over and patted her hand. "We're just not compatible people. Lucinda's going to move back into her old condo next week. The timing was really good—her tenant's moving out, so she won't have to look for a place to stay. She's going to go back to work. I think she's missed working."

Lucinda had been a costume designer for the film and television industry.

"Then have her get a job, but don't split up." Chloe had to make him understand. "You and Lucinda are perfect for each other. You can't get a divorce—you'll be miserable apart. Jeez, Dad, don't you remember how lonely you were before you and Lucinda got together?"

"Chloe, you don't understand," he said. "Loneliness is the worst reason there is for two people to stay together."

"I'm not saying that's why you should stay to-

gether,'' she argued. ''You ought to be together because you love each other. I'm only saying that before
you married Lucinda you'd become a workaholic because you were so alone.''

''Nonsense,'' he said brusquely. ''I always had you
here.''

But that wasn't true, she thought. She'd never bothered to stay home and keep him company. She'd spent
most of her free time shopping or getting her hair
done or doing something else equally stupid.

''Don't worry, kiddo,'' he continued heartily, ''I
won't make the same mistakes I made before; I won't
spend every night and weekend at the office. I've
learned that's no way to live your life.''

''You learned that because Lucinda taught you
there was something better. Since you married her
you've taken up hiking and sailing and going to movies again. . . .''

''Chloe, stop it,'' he ordered. ''I know you mean
well, but this has nothing to do with you.''

''Nothing to do with me?'' she yelped. ''You can't
be serious. This is my fault, I'm the one that kept
driving the wedges between the two of you. I was the
one that kept at you about her, always pointing out
her faults, always looking for the worst. You can't
just give up on this marriage, you just can't.''

''Honey.'' He slashed through the air with his
hand. ''Give it up—it's over. Lucinda and Nick will
be out of here next weekend.'' He pushed back from
the table, got up, and stalked out of the dining room.

Stunned and heartsick, she continued to sit at the
table and stare blindly out the window. For once, the

spectacular view of the lights of Landsdale left her cold.

She didn't know what to do next. Because of her father's announcement, she hadn't finished telling them her own stuff, but that wasn't important to her anymore. She'd pretty much come to the conclusion that no one was going to believe her anyway. But she had to do something about her father and Lucinda.

Her father was wrong. The breakup was her fault and her fault alone. She'd actively worked against them from the moment Lucinda moved in. If she'd kept her big nose out of things, the two of them would have been happy.

Carlotta bustled into the room. She had a large, empty tray in her hand. She stopped when she saw Chloe just sitting there. "You okay?"

"I'm fine," she replied quickly. She got up and reached for the tray.

Carlotta brushed her aside and moved briskly to the table. She began to clear. "I don't know what you think you're doin'," she said as she stacked the plates on the tray, "but thanks. I do want to be with Elvira as much as I can."

Chloe reached for the heavy fajita platter. "It's all right—it's the least I can do. You should have been having all your weekends off all along."

"You don't have to do that." Carlotta nodded at the plate Chloe held. "I can clean up."

"I'll help," Chloe insisted. "It's about time I learned where the dishwasher is."

•   •   •

By the time they'd cleared up the dining room and kitchen, the house was deathly quiet. Carlotta, who'd shown remarkable patience in instructing Chloe on how to scrape plates and load a dishwasher, had gone to her room.

Chloe wandered outside and onto the wide terrace. She walked toward the shadows of the lawn, away from the glow of the lights from the pool and the Jacuzzi. Stopping by a heavy redwood bench, she looked up at the stars.

For a brief moment, she forgot her troubles as she lost herself in the beauty of the night sky. Despite her concern about Lucinda and her dad, she drank in the loveliness eagerly. She was so glad to be alive that even just the act of breathing was something to be enjoyed and savored.

Her neck began to ache from looking up and reluctantly, she sat down and tried to figure out what to do next. If her father and Lucinda really wanted to divorce, she had no right to interfere. But they didn't really want to split up. She knew that; she could sense it. Just as she could sense that the volunteer who had wheeled her out of the hospital today was a good person and loved helping people. They were splitting up because of her, and she had to do something. She had to make it right.

There were a lot of things she had to make right.

Chloe closed her eyes, and the memory of what happened in the ambulance filled her mind. Each and every little detail. Only now she wasn't confused.

She'd closed her eyes in the ambulance, too, even though the paramedics had been trying to talk to her, trying to keep her awake. She'd closed her eyes anyway and that's when all the monitors had lit up like Christmas lights and buzzers had blasted and beeped and screamed for attention.

She hadn't been in the least scared, but all that noise had sure spurred the paramedics into action. She'd floated up to the ceiling of the ambulance and watched them try to bring her back. It had been vaguely interesting, but not frightening.

She hadn't been scared when she started down the tunnel either. At first it had been dark, so dark a color that it wasn't even black, but another, deeper hue that had no word to describe it. Then she'd seen the light. It was small as a pinprick and far away. But even from a distance she'd felt the power.

Indescribable peace.

Indescribable love.

As she'd floated down the tunnel, she'd been flooded with feelings of bliss. Of love. Ideas and certainties had formed in her mind with crystal clarity. All the mysteries had been solved. All the questions answered. She knew why she was here. Why all of them were here. She didn't understand exactly how she knew, but she did.

Right before she'd stepped into the light, she'd been yanked back.

But she'd been changed forever.

CHAPTER THREE

Opening her eyes, Chloe sighed and gave herself a small shake. She was different now, she knew it. She also knew she was going to have a horrible time convincing anyone else. But that wasn't important now. What was important was finding a way to convince her father and Lucinda that they were making a big mistake.

She couldn't do it alone. She needed help. But who?

She glanced up, her gaze catching the light coming from Nick's window. Nick didn't live with them permanently. He had a room in one of the dorms at the University of California at Santa Barbara. On most weekends, vacations, and holidays, he worked at his uncle's ranch. He either slept there or came home late at night. He wasn't around much. That was her fault too. She'd gone out of her way to be less than welcoming when their parents had gotten married. Chloe cringed in mortification as she remembered her little snippy digs at Lucinda and Nick, how she'd never missed an opportunity to imply they were a couple of gold diggers. No wonder Nick had fled to a dorm room. He thought she was the worst kind of spoiled brat. Nothing she could do was going to change his opinion.

But he loved his mother.

If Chloe could just make him see that it was her fault that Lucinda and Dan were splitting up, maybe he'd help.

But even if he did agree to help, what could they do? Chloe frowned. There had to be something. If her interference had caused the breakup, then maybe her interference now could stop it.

Besides, she told herself as she started for the house, maybe if he helped her keep their folks together, she could ask him to help her with her other problem. Not that it was a real problem, she thought as she opened the heavy glass patio doors and stepped inside. She'd eventually figure it out herself. But it sure would be nice to have someone to talk to about it. Too bad she'd been such a witch at school that she didn't have many friends. There was always Mia, of course. Mia was still her friend.

But she didn't think Mia was up to helping her figure out the other thing she'd learned from her trip down the tunnel. Mia was a nice person, and really, really smart, too. Mia always had her nose stuck in a book or a magazine, and she was a whiz on the computer. But Chloe suspected she needed someone with a bit more philosophy in their resume to help her out.

She pushed those thoughts aside and hurried up the stairs. The master bedroom suite was to the left of the staircase. As Chloe passed, she could hear the faint sound of the news on the television. Lucinda was a news freak—every time something happened in the world, she practically glued herself to CNN. Her father, on the other hand, always listened to music and read in bed. That meant her stepmother was probably occupying the bedroom alone. She guessed her father had moved into his study downstairs. It was not only huge, but it had a full bath off it and the couch turned into a queen-sized bed.

She continued down the hall, past guest rooms, bathrooms, and an open area with a couch and two chairs that no one ever sat in, to the very end. His was the last door. The smallest room. She grimaced— she'd been responsible for that too.

Her father had suggested Nick take the room next to hers. It was big, was beautifully furnished, and had a masculine touch to its decoration. There was even a full-sized desk which would have been handy for Nick's books and computer. But she'd objected. She forgot now what kind of lame excuse she'd come up with to keep Nick out, but she'd had one.

She shook her head—she'd have to atone for that later. Right now, she had to persuade him to help her. Lifting her hand, she rapped softly against his door.

Nick stuck his head out. His mouth curled in a sneer when he saw who it was. "What do you want?"

"I've got to talk to you," she said. "Come on, let me in. It's important."

"I think you've done enough talking," he hissed. "Maybe you can con your old man into thinking you're all sweetness and light now, but it'll take more than that little scene you pulled tonight to convince me you've changed.''

Chloe didn't want to stand there all night arguing with him. Nothing she could say was going to make him believe she'd changed, so she didn't even bother trying. Instead, she got right to the heart of the matter. ''It's about your mother. Let me in.''

He drew back and hesitated. Finally, he grudgingly opened the door. ''Okay, come in and say your piece.''

Relieved that she'd gotten past the first hurdle, Chloe dashed inside before he could change his mind. The room was small enough to fit into her closet. There was a twin bed, a tiny entertainment unit with Nick's beat-up old CD player and a thirteen-inch color TV, a small desk and chair draped with Nick's clothes, and a closet with mirrored doors. A backpack, a stack of books, and a heap of dirty laundry spilled out of the open closet.

Nick closed the door, leaned against it, and folded his arms over his chest. ''You've got two minutes.''

Chloe decided he wasn't going to ask her to sit down. She stood in the center of the room. ''It's my fault that your mom and my father are divorcing.''

He raised his eyebrows. ''Well, duh. Tell me something I don't know. You've been a real bitch.''

''Yeah, yeah, I know, so you can save the insults.'' Her hand shot up in a gesture of impatience. ''I know exactly how I behaved and even though you don't believe me, I'm really sorry for it. But that's not important now. What is important is trying to come up with some way to keep them together.''

"And I'm supposed to believe that you're telling the truth now? That you really want them to stay together?"

"Yeah."

"Right," he said sarcastically. "Let me see, you've tried to bust them up since the day they got hitched and now all of a sudden, you're Little Miss Matchmaker?"

"I don't want them to get a divorce," she insisted. Jeez, this was beginning to get boring. "How many more ways do I have to say it? I want them to stay together."

Nick eyed her suspiciously. "Why? Give me a reason, Chloe. A reason to believe you. And don't give me any of that bull about you dying or any crap like that. Just give it to me straight."

"You want a reason? All right—I want them to stay married because they love each other," she shot back, "and I'm not always going to be around for my dad. He needs someone. Someone like your mom. Lucinda's a really good person. She's perfect for him."

"Okay," he said grudgingly. "Let's say that I'm willing to believe you. I'm not exactly saying that," he amended quickly. "But let's say I'm willing to give you the benefit of the doubt. How do I know you're serious about wanting to help?"

"Would I be in here groveling for your help if I wasn't?"

"Okay," he finally replied after a long, considering pause, "I'll help. But I want you to understand something. I'm not doing it because I think you give a crap about my mom, I'm doing it because scary as it is, I actually agree with you. Your old man's a hardnose, but he loves my mom and she loves him. She's had enough grief in her life; I want her to be happy. But don't think for one minute that I'm buying your little number. You haven't changed, Chloe, you just want people to think you have. But you can't fool me. I'll be keeping my eye on you.''

''I don't care about that—I know I don't have any right to expect anyone to believe me.'' Chloe's whole body relaxed in relief. ''But I do want your help. I really don't want them to divorce.''

''So you have any ideas?'' he asked.

''I was hoping you did,'' Chloe replied hesitantly.

''Me?'' He laughed incredulously. ''Come on, you're the schemer in this house, not me.''

She winced. Much as she'd have liked to argue the point, he was right. She was a schemer. ''Give me a day or two to come up with something,'' she finally said. ''Do you know when your mom is actually planning on moving out?''

''Not till next weekend,'' he replied. ''Our old condo won't be empty till then.''

Lucinda and Nick had lived in a condominium complex in the Hollywood Hills until she'd married Dan Marlowe.

''That means we've got less than a week to come up with something,'' Chloe muttered.

Chloe was awakened the next morning by the sound of knocking. Groggily, she opened her eyes and realized the horrible pounding was coming from her door. She stumbled over, opened the door a crack, and peeked out.

Nick stood there. "Hurry up," he ordered. "It's getting late. I've got to get to my uncle's soon, so I don't have a lot of time to waste."

"What are you talking about?" she grumbled as she wiped the sleep from her eyes. Drat, she'd been having this really great dream, too.

He rolled his eyes. "A plan, champ. What have you come up with?"

"Come on in and we'll talk about it," she said, yawning widely. "I'll just throw on a robe." Not that she needed one—her granny nightie covered her from head to toe.

Nick shuddered. "It's way too early in the morning to face your room. Get dressed and I'll meet you down in the kitchen. Everyone's gone. Your dad's at work, Mom went to a meeting at Paramount, and Carlotta's shopping."

"Give me five minutes," Chloe agreed. She closed the door and headed for the bathroom. She didn't think her room was *that* bad. A little elaborate, maybe, but not completely tacky. She stood and surveyed her kingdom.

The walls were a pale, cream color which went nicely with the thick, maroon carpet. Pink lace coverings, far too elaborate to be mere curtains, were draped over and around the huge windows opposite the bed. There was a padded window seat with huge pink, maroon, and white cushions, a white armoire, and a tall, matching chest of drawers, both with gold handles. On the far side of the room was her lace-canopied bed. Next to that was her bathroom and on the other side of the bathroom door was a mirrored walk-in closet filled with enough clothes to outfit a third-world country.

Nick was sipping coffee when she hurried into the kitchen. "Wonders never cease—you're actually on time," he drawled sarcastically.

"You said you were in a hurry," she muttered. "I didn't think the occasion called for formal dress." She'd brushed her teeth and pulled on a pair of jeans and a T-shirt. "Can I have some of that?" She pointed to his cup.

"Since when did you start drinking coffee?"

"I just thought I'd like to try it," she said. "It smells good." She went to the counter, opened one of the cupboards, and pulled down a mug. Since her experience, she'd found she was intensely interested in trying lots of things. "Life's short," she heard herself murmur. "I want to do it all."

Taking her coffee, she went over and plopped down on the stool opposite him. "Okay, what have you come up with?" she asked hopefully.

"Not much," he said. "I was hoping you'd come up with an idea."

"I do kinda have an idea," she admitted. "But it's sort of dumb."

"Lots of your ideas are dumb," he replied, "but they've worked."

Chloe wasn't sure if she'd been insulted or complimented. "True. Okay. I was thinking that your mom decided to leave now because your condo's going to be empty, right?"

Nick thought for a moment. "I'm not sure. Things got pretty tense between Mom and Dan after you pulled that little number with the check. I think she'd have left that night, only you took off and wrapped your car around a tree."

Chloe winced inwardly. "I guess my question is if your mom didn't have the condo, would she be moving out right now?"

"Probably not," Nick said. "She's determined not to take any money from your dad and she doesn't have the money for a new place. You know, first and last months' rent, a security deposit. Getting someplace decent in L.A. costs a bundle. Mom hasn't worked since she married Dan so she doesn't have anything saved."

Chloe nodded. Maybe her idea wasn't as far-fetched as she'd first thought. "What about her job prospects? Any good?"

"She's at the studio as we speak." Nick grinned proudly. "With her track record, she'll probably have something lined up by next week." He put his cup down and leaned back. "Okay, give. What's up? What are you planning?"

"Well, it seems to me that if Lucinda didn't have anyplace to go for a month or two, she'd have to stay here."

"Chloe," Nick interrupted. "Reality check. Mom does have some place to go. Her condo, remember? Her tenants are moving out because they can't make the rent."

"But what if they could make their rent?" she persisted.

"It wouldn't make any difference. It might delay them leaving for a month. . . ."

"That's all we'd need," Chloe exclaimed. "A lot can happen in a month. Especially as we'll be working to bring them together."

"As opposed to your previous efforts to bust them up," he mused.

"It'll work, Nick," she said earnestly. "I know it'll work."

"Okay, for argument's sake, let's say you're right. We've still got a major problem on our hands. Tina lost her job on the soap opera three months ago and Jason hasn't had a part in over a year. They can't pay the rent."

"Where are they going?"

"Probably up to their place in Big Bear," he said. "It's not like Mom's throwing them out, you know."

"I wasn't implying she was."

"They're friends of hers," he insisted. "They're the ones who called her and said they were moving. Mom isn't a monster—she wouldn't have tossed them out into the street."

"I'm sure your mom wouldn't have thrown them out," Chloe said quickly. Jeez, Nick was really touchy about some things. "But it's good they're friends of your mom." She couldn't believe her luck. "I didn't know that."

Nick rolled his eyes. "Of course you didn't know it. You never listen to anything that isn't about you. The Everetts are Mom's best friends."

"Have I met them?"

He sighed, and Chloe wished she hadn't asked. But she was trying to put faces to names.

"Tina was the matron of honor at her wedding to your dad," Nick said impatiently. "And Jason was one of the ushers."

"Okay, okay, I'll admit I've been self-centered." Great—was he going to be rubbing her nose in it all the time? "But that's not important now. What is is that the Everetts will want to help, right?"

"What are you talking about? Mom needs the rent money. Even if Tina and Jason wanted to help, they couldn't. They're broke," he stated flatly. "I know it's an alien concept for you, but *they have no money.*"

"I know what broke is," she said irritably. "But we could give them the money. Understand? We could pay the rent for them."

"With what?" he shouted. "I've got enough in the bank for my tuition and that's it. I'll probably have to be bunking at my uncle's place and commuting this year to school. Things are tight. So unless you've got a stash of cash, you can count me out."

She didn't and her allowance, generous as it was, wasn't due till the first of October. But she wasn't giving up. There had to be a way. She opened her mouth and shut it just as fast. Nick was glaring into his coffee mug; his face had gone red. It took her a minute to understand what was going on.

He was embarrassed because he was broke. Good grief, she didn't expect him to be rolling in money. He was a college student. But she had a feeling that if she said anything along those lines, she'd just make things worse. Of course she'd make it worse. She winced, remembering all the times she'd needled him about not having cash. No wonder he couldn't stand her. Well, rats, she thought, now there was another thing to put on her atonement list. A list that was getting longer by the minute. If she said the wrong thing, she'd really screw things up.

"Yeah, I'm busted too," she finally muttered. "And considering what I did to the car, I don't think Dad's going to float me a loan."

It was apparently the right thing to say, because Nick actually laughed. For once, it wasn't one of those sneering, nasty laughs of his, either. It was a real one. "Yeah, Princess, you shoulda stayed in that coma a couple more days. Given him long enough to really freak over whether or not you were going to make it."

Chloe thought about their dilemma. "How much do we need?"

"For the rent?" His eyebrows shot up. "Thirteen hundred."

"Dollars!"

"I ain't talkin' pesos here," he replied. "It's too bad, too. I think your idea might have worked. Mom probably would stay on if Tina and Jason could swing the rent. Your dad doesn't want her to leave."

"How do you know?" Chloe hadn't even considered that possibility.

"I overheard them last night after you'd gone to bed."

"You were eavesdropping again," she yelped.

"Not deliberately," he protested. "Believe me,

they were screaming at each other loud enough to raise the dead.''

''That's good,'' she said. ''I mean, that he doesn't want her to leave. It'll make it easier for us.''

Nick's mouth dropped open. ''Chloe, are you deaf? Don't you get it? It won't work.''

''You just said you thought it was a good idea,'' she persisted.

''Only if we had thirteen hundred bucks.''

''There's got to be a way,'' Chloe insisted. She wasn't going to give up. She wasn't going to let her actions bring such misery and heartbreak to her father or his mother.

She closed her eyes for a moment, willing herself to think. What did people do when they needed money fast? They cashed in their savings . . . but she couldn't touch her savings bonds, and to get to her account at the bank she needed her father's counter-signature because she wasn't of age. Hell, sometimes it was a real pain being seventeen. Suddenly, an image popped into her head.

''I've got it,'' she cried. ''The pig. We'll bust open the pig.''

''Pig?'' Nick looked at her like she'd lost it. ''What pig?''

She jumped off the stool and grabbed his hand, then dropped it just as quickly as he frowned. ''Get a hammer and meet me in my room,'' she said excitedly to cover her embarrassment.

Nick got up, his expression puzzled. ''Okay, but I hope you're not going to get us both in trouble.''

"Hurry," she called over her shoulder as she raced for the stairway.

When Nick and the hammer came into her room a few minutes later, she was on her knees pulling a huge, fat, ceramic pig out of the depths of her walk-in closet.

"Give me a hand with this," she panted, giving the front legs a hard pull. "It weighs a ton."

"What the . . ." Nick tossed the hammer on the bed and crossed over to Chloe. "I've seen microwave ovens smaller than that thing." He leaned down, picked it up, and then quickly put it back down. "What's in here? Gold bars?"

"Silver dollars, half dollars, and quarters," she said, pulling it farther into her room. "It's the genuine article. A real piggy bank. My parents got it for me when I was really little. I'd forgotten all about it. There's got to be a ton of money in here. It's almost full."

"You want to break it open?" he asked incredulously.

"That's the idea," Chloe replied.

Between the two of them they maneuvered it next to the bed. She leaned up on her knees, spotted the hammer, and grabbed it. Raising it over her head, she started to bring it down onto porky's fat back when Nick suddenly lunged forward.

"Not like that!" he yelped, yanking the handle out of her hands. "Dammit, you're going to have glass everywhere."

Chloe stared at him for a moment. "Then how? I want this thing busted open. We need that cash."

Nick sat back on his heels and stared at her. "You're really serious, aren't you?"

"Of course I am," she replied. She sighed. "What's it going to take to get you to believe me? A blood oath?"

"That'd do for starters," he replied, "but for now, why don't we find a big towel. Something to wrap this porker in so you don't spray both of us with glass. I don't need a bloodbath."

"Okay, be right back." Chloe laughed, delighted that he was finally getting with the program. She jumped to her feet and dashed into her bathroom. From the linen closet next to the oversized tub, she took out a beach towel and ran back to her room.

Nick jerked his chin down toward the carpet next to porky. "Spread it out and we'll roll the little sucker onto it."

She flattened the towel and helped him scoot the bank onto it. Nick carefully wrapped the edges of the towel around the porcelain and then picked up the hammer. "You want me to do it?"

She hesitated. She kinda wanted to do it herself. How often in life did you get a real chance to smash the hell out of something? But from the look of anticipation on his face, she could tell he really wanted to let loose with the hammer. "By all means," she said with a flourish. "Do the honors."

Nick grinned, pulled back, and let it rip. The sound of shattering porcelain was muted by the towel, but not much. Chloe was glad they were the only ones in the house.

He put the hammer down and flipped back the

edges of the towel. In front of them were heaps and heaps of silver coins, intermingled with broken ceramic. Chloe began digging out the change.

"Hey, be careful," Nick warned as he yanked her hand away. "You're going to cut yourself that way. Let's do this right. Let's pick all the glass out first and then count it systematically."

It took them a good fifteen minutes before they were ready to start counting. "We could take all the change down to the supermarket," Chloe suggested. "They have one of those counting machines there."

"They take a fee," Nick pointed out. He was stacking silver dollars into neat piles of ten dollars each.

"Yeah," she admitted as she continued stacking quarters. "But it would be a lot faster than this."

"If we're going to do this, we're going to need all the cash we can lay our hands on. We can't afford to give up any of it. Besides, this won't take much longer," he said.

He was wrong about that. To Chloe, it seemed like it was taking hours, but eventually the floor was covered with neatly stacked piles of change.

Nick, who was far more systematic than Chloe, soon had the piles organized into batches of twenty-five and then fifty dollars. When they'd stacked all the coins, he counted them out. Three times. Then he sat back on his heels and announced, "There's seven hundred twenty-two dollars and seventy-five cents. By my reckoning, that means we're five hundred seventy-seven dollars and twenty-five cents short." He shook his head. "Too bad you busted open the pig."

"No it's not." Chloe wasn't about to let anything

stop her. She dusted the grime off her hands, got to her feet, and went to her armoire. Opening the top drawer, she rummaged inside until she found what she needed.

"We're not giving up. We've got these," she said, tossing two velvet jewelry boxes onto the rug. She knelt down next to Nick. "They're worth something."

Curious, he picked up the one nearest him and opened it. "It's a watch," he said.

"It's a Rolex," she corrected. "Dad bought it for me a couple of years ago. We should get a bundle for it." She picked up the other box and opened it. "And we've got this, too." She waved a flashy pin in the shape of a four-leaf clover under his nose. "The outer leaves are diamonds and the inside gem is a ruby. This has got to be worth something too. Dad bought it two years ago for my fifteenth birthday."

Nick shook his head in confusion. "Chloe, this is all real nice. But what are you thinking? You can't take this stuff back to the store and get cash for it. Not if your dad bought them that long ago."

Chloe closed her eyes and sighed. She didn't blame Nick for jumping to that conclusion. She was notorious for returning presents. She thought back to this past Christmas, to the disappointed look on her father's face when he'd found out she'd returned the expensive coat he'd bought her and kept the cash instead. She remembered the hurt in his eyes, and even the look of disappointment in Lucinda's. She'd been a selfish jerk again, concerned only with getting what she wanted instead of being grateful that someone had gotten her a present. "I'm not taking it back to the store."

"Then how are you planning on getting any money?" he challenged.

"Easy," she replied. "I'll take them to a pawnshop. They pay money for stuff."

"A pawnshop? You?" Nick started to laugh. "You've got to be kidding."

"I don't see what's so funny," she shot back. "We need money. I've got stuff that's worth money. There's a couple of pawnshops over on Twin Oaks Boulevard. I'll go there."

Nick looked amused. He watched her as she picked up the boxes and stuffed them in her purse. "You planning on going by yourself?"

"If I have to," she said. "But I was hoping you'd go with me."

He shook his head. "Chloe, you don't understand. We can't take that stuff over to Twin Oaks Boulevard."

"Why not?"

"For starters, you're not eighteen."

"You are," she pointed out. "You can do it."

Again he shook his head. "No way. It's a woman's watch and a woman's pin. No one on Twin Oaks Boulevard is going to give me a dime for any of it. They'll think it's hot."

"You mean stolen?" Chloe said, disappointed.

"You got it."

"Then what are we going to do?" she demanded. "We can't give up now. Not when we're this close."

"Who said anything about giving up," he said

cheerfully. "We can get that stuff pawned all right, just not here in Landsdale."

"I'll still be underage no matter where we go," she reminded him.

"True, but there's a way around that. Tomorrow, you and I'll take a little trip. There's a pawnshop on Sunset Boulevard that I know. The owner knows me too. He'll take my word that this stuff isn't stolen."

"How does he know you?" she asked curiously. "Have you done this before?" As her tone was not judgmental, but actually somewhat awed, he didn't take offense at the question.

"Mom's in the entertainment industry," he explained. "We've had to pawn stuff a time or two. I'd hoped when she married your old man that those days were behind us. Looks like I was wrong, doesn't it?"

CHAPTER FOUR

Chloe looked away. Now that she understood exactly what the consequences of her earlier behavior meant for Nick and his mother, she felt even more guilty. What else was new? She felt guilty because she *was* guilty. "I'm sorry," Chloe said softly. "I haven't made things easy for you or your mom. I didn't realize what life must have been like for you."

"Who said life was supposed to be easy?" Nick pointed out with a shrug. "Besides, it wasn't that bad. I mean, we only pawned stuff because my mom had to take care of my dad before he died. He was bedridden for over a year. If she'd been able to work, we'd have been okay."

"What did you father die from?" she asked softly. She realized she'd never bothered to ask even the most ordinary of questions about either Nick or Lucinda.

"What else? Cancer." He sighed. "He was a great guy."

"How old were you?"

"Fourteen," he replied. He gazed blankly at the far wall, then gave himself a small shake. "Tomorrow we'll head down to L.A. and see how much we can get for your stuff."

"Why can't we go today?" she asked. "We don't have a lot of time. Your mom's tenants are going to move next week."

"The only way we can get there today is if you've got a transporter beam hidden under your bed. Your car is totaled and mine needs a new set of brakes."

"So? It's still early," she persisted. "There should be plenty of time to get your car fixed. If we get it there right away, they could have it done by—"

"You don't get it, do you?" he interrupted. "I'm broke. I'm not taking it to a shop, I'm doing it myself."

"You're fixing your own brakes?" Chloe asked, rather impressed. She didn't know how to fix anything. For that matter, neither did her dad.

"That's right." He glanced at his watch. "And I'd better get moving. I'm going to have to baby the car all the way to my uncle's place."

"Why can't you fix them here?" she asked. She didn't think her father would care.

Suddenly her door burst open and Mia Coleridge, her best friend, flew into the room. Her short, stocky build was encased in a pair of tight jeans, frayed at the ankles, and a short-sleeved yellow T-shirt. Mia grinned and wiped a dangling blonde curl off her forehead. She skidded to a halt as she knocked over a stack of fifty-cent pieces. "Sorry," she apologized, "I didn't meant to bust in on you. I knocked but no one answered. Your back door was open so I just came on in. Good grief, it looks like you two ripped off a slot machine!'' Bright red patches were spreading upward over her pale cheeks. Chloe knew the blushing was because Mia had a monumental crush on Nick. What was worse, he knew it. But to his credit, he pretended he didn't.

''That's okay,'' Chloe said quickly. ''Come on in and have a seat,'' she said, gesturing at an empty spot on the rug.

''How are you feeling?'' Mia, still blushing, lowered herself down next to the bed.

''Fine,'' Chloe replied cheerfully. ''The doctor gave me a clean bill of health.''

''That's good.'' Mia shot a quick look at Nick. ''Hi. I hope I didn't interrupt anything.''

Nick gave her a devastating smile. One that sent another wave of color washing all the way down to her neck. ''I'm helping the rich girl count her coins,'' he said lightly. ''We busted open her piggy bank.''

Mia nodded. By her expression, it was obvious she was as curious as a cat, but she was far too polite to ask. At least in front of Nick. ''I see. Well, uh, what are you guys doing today?''

''Not much of anything,'' Chloe said. ''Nick and I had some things to take care of, but we won't have any wheels till he gets his brakes fixed.''

''Speaking of which, I'd better get moving.'' Nick shot to his feet. ''Nice seeing you again, Mia. See ya later.''

''It was nice seeing you, too,'' Mia called after him. She turned back to Chloe, her face bright and

her smile wide. "He's such a great guy," she gushed.
"I don't see why you don't like him."

"I like him fine," Chloe said.

"Since when?"

Chloe opened her mouth to reply and then realized
that unless she wanted to go through the whole white
light and tunnel business, she'd better watch her
mouth. "Since I got a little more mature," she said.
It was the best explanation she could come up with
on the spur of the moment.

"Oh." Mia nodded. "I came to see you in the hospital, but they wouldn't let me in your room. You
were still unconscious."

"I know, Nick told me. That was really nice of
you." Chloe was suddenly deeply ashamed of the way
she'd treated her friend in the past. Mia was a genuinely nice person. Smart, too, with a 3.5 GPA. She'd
moved up here from Long Beach last January and
started at Twin Oaks High. It wasn't easy to make
friends when you came into a new school in the mid-
dle of the year; most people already had their friends
by then. Mia lived with her mom in a small apartment
just off Twin Oaks Boulvard—the older, cheaper part
of town. Her clothes and shoes were from discount
stores and she was desperately trying to find a job to
earn money for college. Chloe had treated her like
dirt. Mia had put up with it because she was good-
hearted by nature and because she didn't have anyone
else to hang out with. "But then, you're a really good
person."

Mia's mouth opened in surprise. "Uh, thanks."

"No, really," Chloe persisted. "I'm lucky to have

a friend like you. You're nice and you're kind. You're always doing nice things for people. You know, like helping your neighbor, Mrs. Creedly, with her shopping."

Mia stared at her for a moment and then looked down at the carpet. "Are you making fun of me?"

"No," Chloe protested. Great, even when she tried to be nice people expected the worst from her. But she was determined to make up for the shabby way she'd behaved. "I'm absolutely sincere. You are nice and I am lucky to have a friend like you."

"I'm lucky to have you, too," Mia murmured. She lifted her chin and smiled. "You were the only one willing to hang out with me when I moved here."

"Let's just say we're lucky to have each other." Chloe laughed. Mia's words made her feel a little better. Maybe she hadn't been as awful as she'd thought. "Come on, let's go to the mall. We'll do some window-shopping and then I'll buy you lunch. Oh no, I forgot. I don't have my car. . . ."

"I've got my mom's car," Mia said eagerly. Then her face fell. "Forget it, I know you don't like being seen in that old . . . but I could park at the other end of the lot."

Chloe bit her lip, remembering how she'd refused to ride in Mia's mother's little compact because it was too uncool. "Wheels are wheels, Mia. Besides, I was being a class A wench before. You're mom's car is fine. It runs, doesn't it. You park wherever you want. I'm just grateful you're giving me a ride."

● ● ●

They window-shopped and giggled all the way through the Landsdale Mall. Chloe laughed at Mia's sly wit and Mia, occasionally giving Chloe a wary look, seemed to relax more and more as the morning wore on.

Just after noon they left the mall and went to Harbinger's, a local coffee shop where all the kids from Landsdale High hung out. Chloe pulled the door open for them and they stepped inside. Her mouth watered at the scent of french fries and sizzling burgers.

"It's packed," Mia murmured. She edged behind Chloe, almost as though she was trying to hide. "Oh no, there's Shawna. She's coming this way."

The tall, pretty blonde heading straight for them was Chloe's former best friend. Shawna Follan's family was even wealthier than Chloe's dad. The two girls had had a falling-out at the junior prom last May. They hadn't really been friends since then.

"Chloe," Shawna cried. "I heard about your accident. God, how awful. I was so worried."

"I'm fine," Chloe volunteered. "How have you been?" She suspected the only reason Shawna had busted her buns to talk to her now was to find out all the gory details about the accident. She'd always been a bit of a ghoul.

"Oh, let's not talk about me," Shawna said. "I want to hear all about what happened. Did you really total your car?"

"It's pretty messed up."

"I heard you died," Shawna continued dramatically. "Is it true? Did you see the white light? Did you go down the tunnel? Was your mother waiting on the other side?''

Chloe wasn't going to talk about it with Shawna. ''You've been watching too much TV, Shawna,'' she said with a laugh. ''But thanks for asking. Come on, Mia, let's get a booth.''

''You can join us,'' Shawna offered quickly. Chloe noticed she didn't even look at Mia when she made the offer. ''We're right over there.'' She pointed to one of the big booths on the far side of the lunch counter. ''Everyone would like to see you.''

All her old friends were there. Andrew Barrows, the local, self-appointed blond-haired surf god was sitting next to Lydia Parks, last year's junior prom queen. Across from them was Wesley Marton, the quarterback for the Landsdale High School football team. Lydia caught her eye and waved gaily. Andrew nodded and even Winston unbent enough to waggle his fingers at her. These people were her friends. Yet none of them had called or come by after the accident. Not once. Not even to see how she was doing.

Maybe she wasn't such a great person, she thought, but neither were any of them. At least she'd woken up in time, so to speak, to learn what was important. ''Some other time, Shawna,'' she said. ''I'm still a little tired from the accident. Too much stimulation isn't good for me. And Mia and I have a lot of things we need to talk about.''

Shawna gaped at her, her expression clearly incredulous. ''Suit yourself. If you'd rather go slumming''— she looked pointedly at Mia—''it's no skin off my nose.''

Chloe's eyes narrowed angrily. She didn't mind people taking shots at her—she deserved it. But Mia didn't. "No, Shawna, you don't understand. If I'd gone with you and my so-called friends, then it would be slumming. Friends at least pick up the phone to check on how someone's doing when they've done the coma and ambulance thing." With that, she turned on her heel and started for the back of the diner. There were always empty booths in the back. Mia, her face crimson, hurried after her.

"You didn't have to do that," Mia hissed. "I'd have understood if you wanted to have lunch with your friends."

"Those guys aren't my friends." Chloe slid into a booth. "They're just people I've known since kindergarten. You're my friend, Mia. You're the one who came to see me. You're the one who showed up today to see how I was doing. I haven't heard one word from any of them. Oh, don't get me wrong, they're not bad people. Not at all. They're just like the way I used to be, totally self-centered."

"You're not totally self-centered," Mia said, but she was grinning broadly.

Chloe grinned back at her and picked up the menu. She gave it a cursory glance and then snapped it shut as the waitress came to take their order. "I'll have a cheeseburger, fries, and a root beer."

"I'll have the same," Mia echoed. "Thanks for defending me back there," she said as soon as they were alone. "Shawna's always scared me a little."

"Shawna scares everyone," Chloe replied. "But you know what, she's not really all that hot. I think that for a moment back there she was even a little ashamed. Look, Mia, I was being straight with you before. You've been a good friend to me and I've treated you lousy. I'm sorry, really sorry, and I promise I'll never do it again.''

Mia regarded her thoughtfully for a moment. ''You're serious, aren't you?''

''Dead serious,'' Chloe said. ''But I won't get mad if you don't believe me. I mean, I've changed. But I'll understand if you don't want to take my word for it. No one else has.''

· Mia eyed her speculatively, as though she was deciding on whether or not Chloe needed to go to a shrink. ''I believe you,'' she finally said, but her voice lacked conviction. ''I mean, you're being really nice and you don't have to. What happened, Chloe?''

Chloe hesitated, unsure of whether or not she ought to tell anyone about what had happened to her in the ambulance. But then she realized it didn't really matter—if Shawna and her crowd knew about it, it must be all over town. She suddenly realized she wanted to talk about it with Mia. ''Well, it's going to sound weird.''

''That's okay, I like weird.''

''I'm not exactly sure where to start.''

''Try the beginning,'' Mia suggested as she removed the straw from its wrapper and stuck it in her glass. ''That's what Mom always makes me do. I take it this transformation had something to do with your accident?''

''Yeah.'' Chloe stuck her straw in the root beer and took a long, deep sip.

"Then the gossip really is true? You died?"

Chloe nodded. "Yup. Sure did."

"Wow." Mia's eyes grew as big as saucers. "Tell me what happened and don't leave out any of the details. Start with you being in your car."

"Well, I was driving down Camden Road."

"How fast were you going?"

"Too fast," Chloe admitted. "I was really pissed. Nick had reamed me out so I was outta there like you wouldn't believe. I wasn't going anywhere in particular, I just wanted to get away from the house." She stopped as she saw the waitress bringing them their order.

"Would you like anything else?" she asked as she put the food in front of them.

"No, this'll do it," Chloe said. Automatically, she reached for the ketchup bottle from the side of the table, while Mia snatched up the salt shaker. Both girls doused their food and fiddled with their burgers till they had them just the way they liked.

"Okay," Mia ordered as she lifted her burger to her lips. "Go on. You'd taken off because you were pissed off at Nick."

"Right." Chloe popped a fry in her mouth. "Anyway, I was hitting it pretty hard up Camden Road. All of a sudden, the car spun out of control and I went flying into a tree. I cracked my head good on the steering wheel."

"Why did you lose control of the car?" Mia asked.

"I guess because of the speeding . . . because I was going too fast." Frowning, Chloe broke off. Had she been speeding? All of a sudden, she wasn't so sure as an image of the speedometer popped into her head. "No, maybe I wasn't. . . . I don't know. I think I was only doing about thirty-five."

"That's not too fast for Camden Road," Mia said. "It's dead straight. But for argument's sake, let's say that's why you flew into the tree. What happened then?"

Chloe frowned again. "I'm not sure. The next thing I remember is hearing the sirens and then the ambulance coming. I was real woozy. But I remember being lifted onto the gurney and being put in it. I kept thinking that my dad was really going to be mad when he saw the car."

"But all you had was a concussion, right?"

"That's what the doctor claims." Chloe's mouth was suddenly dry so she took a sip from her soda. "But something happened when I was in the ambulance. I remember finding myself floating on the ceiling, looking down at my body. I wasn't scared at the time; I wasn't even worried. Actually, it was pretty interesting."

Mia straightened like a puppet getting its string pulled. "Wow! You're really serious, right?"

"Would I kid about something like that? But the weird thing is, I can remember what was happening the whole time I was dead. I mean, I can see it all, every little detail. I can tell you what the paramedics did, what they said to each other, everything."

"Did you go down the tunnel?" Mia asked eagerly. "Did you see the white light?"

"How do you know that?" It was the same question Shawna asked, but for some reason, Chloe didn't mind talking about it to Mia.

"Because I've read about this stuff. They're called Near Death Experiences," Mia explained. "They're actually pretty common. Some people think they're genuine spiritual experiences."

"It *was* genuine," Chloe argued.

"I'm not saying it wasn't," Mia replied. "But keep an open mind. There is a scientific point of view about it too."

"Which is?"

"The scientific point of view is simply that the perception of the light and the feeling of peace is just your brain shutting down. It's like nature's way of letting you out easy." Mia shook her head. "Wow. You actually died. What does your old man think?"

"That the paramedics screwed up and we ought to sue," Chloe mumbled.

"Doesn't he realize you almost pegged out?" Mia's brows drew together. "Isn't he just grateful you're still in the land of the living?"

She shrugged. "He's grateful, I guess. But the whole thing freaked him out pretty badly. He hasn't even asked me any questions about the experience."

"He's probably too scared to talk about it," Mia murmured. "Most of us don't like to think about death, let alone ask questions."

Chloe sighed. She knew what had happened. She knew she was different. "Do you believe me?"

"Of course I do," Mia declared.

"You do?"

"Yup." Mia nodded. "To be honest, you don't

have the imagination to dig up a story like this. Why would you bother? It can't be because you want more attention—you get plenty of that already. Besides''— she leaned closer—"there is something kinda different about you. I can see it in you face. It's softer, and, well, nicer.''

"Thanks, I think." Chloe grinned broadly. She was relieved to finally be able to talk about it. She wondered if she should tell Mia the rest. "Uh, look, there's something else I'd like to tell you.''

"You mean there's more?'' Mia took another bite of her burger.

"Yeah. Ever since it happened, well, I've had these weird feelings. . . .'' Chloe began.

"You mean like you want to be nice and stuff like that?''

"That's part of it,'' Chloe replied. "I mean, I feel like I've got to make up for all the really awful things I've done to people—''

"That's normal,'' Mia interrupted.

"Really?''

"There's been lots of magazine articles and books about it. *Oprah* even did a show on it.'' Mia polished off the last of her fries.

Chloe nodded slowly. It wasn't that she doubted her friend, but she was curious as to Mia's source of knowledge. She decided to find out as much as she could about her experience. Especially now that she knew others had had it. "Where can I get these books?''

"We'll go to the library later if you want,'' Mia replied. "It should be pretty easy to look up.''

"Good. Let's go as soon as we eat. I really need to find out more," she said and pushed her plate to one side.

Nick rolled out from underneath his Chevy and reached for the clean rag he'd laid next to his toolbox. Sitting up, he stared at the corral next to the barn as he absently cleaned the grease off his fingers. His uncle Bobby was walking one of the horses, talking softly to the skittish animal as he walked her around the ring.

He tossed the rag to one side and got to his feet. It had taken the better part of the day, but his brakes were fixed. Nick lovingly patted the front fender of his beat-up compact. Despite the flaking paint and the primer spots on the front door, the car was his pride and joy. He'd bought it as an old junk heap two days after his sixteenth birthday. With his uncle's help and several hundred hours of hard work, the car was now as mechanically sound as anything that rolled off an assembly line in Detroit. It would get them to L.A. tomorrow.

Nick frowned as he remembered the reason for tomorrow's errand. She'd better be on the level with this, he told himself as he picked up his toolbox and tossed it in the trunk. He didn't want his mom jerked around just because little Chloe had some kind of burr up her butt.

Nick sighed and closed the trunk door. What if Chloe was faking it? What if she hadn't changed? What if this trip to the pawnshop and her crazy idea to patch up his mom and her dad's marriage was all part of some psycho plan she had to mess up his mom's life once and for all.

Chloe was capable of anything.

She was the perfect schemer. God, she was worse than one of those chicks on that soap opera Tina used to be on. What if she was still the same selfish, obnoxious little bitch she'd been since he'd met her? Then what?

Then he'd wring her neck, that's what, he promised himself as he tested the door to make sure it had closed firmly. He grimaced guiltily as he thought about Chloe. It was his fault that she'd wrecked her car. They'd had one hell of an argument that morning. But what had she expected? She'd come prancing out with her nose in the air because she thought she'd finally convinced her father that his mom was some kind of gold-digging thief.

He'd lost his temper, called Chloe a few choice names and reduced her to tears. She'd taken off like a bat out of hell and an hour later, they'd gotten the call from the hospital. "It wasn't my fault," he mumbled. "She's always driven too fast."

"What wasn't your fault?"

Nick whirled around. "Uncle Bobby. I thought you were still walking Sheeba."

"I let Chris take over. Both of them need the exercise." Bobby Mallory was a tall, middle-aged man with a weather-beaten face, ginger-colored hair sprinkled with gray at the temples, and twinkling blue eyes. Since his brother's death, he'd been a second father to Nick. "You okay?"

Nick shrugged. "Yeah, I'm fine."

Bobby nodded. "You get them brake pads on?"

"Yeah." Nick patted the fender again. "She's running like a charm. Uncle Bobby," he asked on impulse, "do you think people can change?"

Bobby didn't seem surprised by the question. Truth was, Nick was fairly sure his uncle had realized something was bugging him and had ambled over to see if he could pry it out. That was Uncle Bobby's way of doing things. He never came right out and asked what was wrong; he just sort of stood around and waited until you felt like talking about it. Not that Nick really felt like talking about Chloe. But he needed his uncle's advice. He couldn't afford to take part in one of Chloe's schemes if that scheme was likely to backfire and hurt his mom.

"Change how?" Bobby asked. "You mean like can they quit smoking or drinking or doing drugs?"

Nick shook his head. Why did adults always assume that a teen's problem involved alcohol, cigarettes, or dope? "No, I mean can they change their character?"

Bobby thought about it for a moment. "If they really want to, they can," he finally said.

"But what about that old saying 'A leopard can't change its spots?' "

"People aren't leopards," Bobby replied easily. "And a leopard's spots are on the outside. Character is something that comes from within."

Nick nodded. Maybe he owed Chloe a chance.

Maybe he didn't have a choice. He wanted his mom to be happy.

But if this was one of Chloe's tricks, he vowed, he'd make her sorry she was ever born.

Chloe and Mia had taken their books and magazines out onto the patio of the library. The hot August sun beat down mercilessly but the library wasn't air-conditioned and the patio was the coolest spot to be found.

Mia had a huge stack of magazines and books on the table in front of her. She was engrossed in her reading, her expression intense as she scanned each and every article she could find about Near Death Experiences. Chloe, on the other hand, not being a particularly fast reader and not being as familiar as Mia with the intricacies of the public library numbering system, had only found one magazine and one newspaper that had anything written about NDEs (as she now called it). She'd read both the article and the newspaper already.

"Are you almost done?" she asked Mia.

Mia raised her hand, but kept on reading. "Just a sec." A few moments later she put down the magazine. Her expression was somber.

"You don't look real happy," Chloe said. "Is something wrong?"

"It's not really wrong," Mia replied hesitantly. "You go first. What did you find out?"

"Well, not much more than I already knew. Floating over your body, tunnel, white light, feelings of love and peace. Feelings that your life has changed dramatically." Chloe shrugged. "I guess that's all there is to it." But there was more. She knew it. She just wasn't sure what it was. "How about you?"

"How can I put this?" Mia stated. "I found out pretty much what you did, except some of the reports that I read claimed that not only had the experience changed them, but that they felt like it had done something else. . . ." She paused. "Oh, how can I put this?"

"Try plain English," Chloe suggested.

"Well, some people had the sense that they'd been sent back for a reason," Mia said hesitantly.

"You mean like they had unfinished business or something?"

"Not exactly," Mia said. "More like they had a strong sense that they'd been sent back to do something. Something important."

"Would patching up a failing marriage be considered important?" Chloe asked.

Mia shrugged. "It's possible. But from what I read, the reason they were sent back was more cosmic than that."

"Cosmic? Like how?"

Mia looked up at the sky, her expression thoughtful. "Generally, I think some people felt they were sent back to do one specific thing. You know, like pull a kid out of the path of a speeding car, something like that. Then the kid they save turns out to be the one that finds the cure for cancer or AIDS or something. That's what some people reported. They feel they were saved for a purpose."

Chloe went absolutely still. Mia was right. She'd been sent back to do something, and it wasn't just to atone for being a class A bitch, either. That's what had been bothering her since she'd regained consciousness in the hospital. That overwhelming sense that she had a purpose to fulfill.

Despite the heat of the summer day, cold chills climbed her spine. She'd been sent back for a reason, a purpose. And once that purpose was fulfilled, her time here would end.

She'd die again, and this time she wouldn't come back.

CHAPTER
FIVE

Lucinda and her dad were in the living room when Mia dropped Chloe off later that afternoon. The way they both shut up when Chloe walked into the living room made it real clear they'd been talking about something serious. Probably their divorce.

"Hi," Chloe said brightly. "Oops, sorry. Looks like I'm interrupting something. Should I leave?"

"That's okay, honey," her father said quickly. "We were finished anyway."

Lucinda gave him a sharp look, made a face, and then started for the hall. "I'll be upstairs," she mumbled.

"Don't go," Chloe cried. "I need to talk to you."

Lucinda stopped and turned. "What is it?"

"I want to apologize," Chloe said softly. She watched her father out of the corner of her eye. "I did a terrible thing to you and I want you to know I'm really sorry. I'll do anything I can to make it up to you."

Lucinda folded her arms over her chest.

"Chloe, you've already apologized for faking that check—you don't have to do it again." Her father laid his hand on her arm.

"No I didn't," Chloe protested. "I tried to the other night, but then you made your grand announcement about the divorce and I didn't get a chance to really tell Lucinda how sorry I am," she told him. She looked back at her stepmother. Lucinda's expression was carefully blank, but there was the glimmer of hope in her eyes. "I can't tell you how rotten I feel about what I did."

"You should feel badly," Lucinda replied. "Forging my name on one of your father's checks was criminal."

"I know," she said, licking her lips, "and I also know it's the reason the two of you are breaking up. That's my fault too. But you've got to believe me, I really, really want you to stay, and I think my dad does too."

Lucinda seemed to hesitate for a moment. "Chloe, I appreciate what you're trying to do, but it's too late. As the saying goes, there's just too much water under the bridge."

"Dinner'll be ready in ten minutes," Carlotta announced from the doorway, "and I could sure use some help settin' the table."

"I'll be right there," Chloe called. She'd apologized half a dozen times now, but this was the first time it had felt right, like she'd actually gotten Lucinda to listen to her. She turned toward the kitchen. As she passed her stepmother, she gave her a wan smile. "I'm really sorry. I wouldn't blame you if you hated me."

Lucinda said nothing.

She and Nick left for Los Angeles bright and early the next morning. Chloe, alone with him in the intimate confines of the small front seat, stared out the window and tried to calm her nerves. She wished she'd been nicer to him. She wished she had the nerve to talk to him about personal things, about what he liked and didn't like, about his friends and school and all the other stuff girls talked to guys about. But she didn't have the guts to say anything. He was only here because he wanted his mother to be happy, not because he liked her at all.

The hot sun beat down on the brown rolling hills as the miles sped by. To avoid commuter traffic, Nick took the county road over to the coast.

Chloe sighed and told herself not to wish for something she could never have. Nick Mallory definitely fit that description. Instead, she forced herself to think about what she'd discovered at the library, the utter certainty that she'd been sent back for a reason. She also thought about what they were doing. Would it work? Would it make any difference at all?

"You're awfully quiet this morning," Nick said as he rolled his window down. "What's up? Having second thoughts?"

"No."

"You sure?" he pressed. "You're going to be parting with a lot of cash and two really valuable pieces."

Chloe sighed. Just once it would be nice if he didn't

think the worst of her. "Give me a break, will you? I'm quiet because I've got a lot on my mind, not because I care about the money or the other stuff."

"Hey, I'm sorry, okay? But you've got to admit, the old Chloe wouldn't have parted with a dime to help someone else."

"Well, I'm not the old Chloe," she snapped. "So for once, stop watching my every move and thinking I'm up to no good."

"Okay, okay." He held up his hand and flashed her a quick grin. "I'll take your word for it. The truth is I feel kinda bad because we're using your money and all."

"Don't feel bad," she protested. "It's my fault your mom's leaving in the first place."

"Yeah, right," he muttered, "there is that."

They arrived in Los Angeles a little after ten o'clock. Nick got off the freeway at Sunset Boulevard and turned west. "We're almost there," he said. "It's just a few more blocks ahead. When we get inside, let me do the talking."

"Okay."

A few minutes later, Nick pulled into an empty space at the end of a block of businesses. Chloe stared out the window at the huge sign over the top of the storefront. *Paradise Pawnshop.* "Interesting name," she muttered as she climbed out of the car.

Nick laughed. "It's the owner's name. John Paradise. My mom and I know him from way back. He was a friend of my dad's."

Chloe gazed at the store curiously. Guitars, flutes, violins, and other instruments were displayed in a large window on one side of the front door. On the other side, there were trays of jewelry, two telescopes sitting on tripods, a raised shelf of video equipment, and one lonely camcorder.

Nick held the door open for her. Chloe, more curious than ever, eagerly stepped inside. Cases filled with rings, watches, microscopes, TVs, computers, stereos, and cameras lined each side of the store. Directly ahead of them, flush against the back wall, was a glass case filled with rifles and guns.

A bearded man dressed in a short-sleeved white polo shirt and khaki pants stood behind a cash register at the back of the store. It happened to be just in front of the gun case. Chloe wondered if that was accidental or not. His sharp face lit up in a smile as he recognized Nick. "Hey, kiddo," he called, "long time no see."

"It's been a while," Nick agreed as he led the way to the counter. He nodded in her direction. "This is my, uh . . . stepsister, Chloe Marlowe."

"Hi." Chloe smiled brightly.

"Nice to meet you. I'm John Paradise." He extended his hand to her and she shook it. "How's your mom these days?" he asked Nick. "I heard she was trying to find a job?"

"She is." Nick nodded.

"If I hear of anything, I'll give her a call," he said.

"Thanks." Nick smiled gratefully. "Uh, look, John, I was wondering if you could help us. We've got some stuff here and we need a loan on it."

"What kind of stuff?" John asked blandly.

"Jewelry and a watch." He nodded at Chloe. She

reached in her purse and pulled out two boxes and laid them on the counter next to the register.

John flipped open the lid on the first box and his eyebrows shot up as he lifted out the broach. "Are these real?"

"Yes," Chloe replied. "The one in the center is a ruby and the others are diamonds. It was a present for my birthday."

He glanced at Chloe. "This is pretty expensive stuff for a kid your age. But then again, I've seen fourteen year olds from Beverly Hills come in here and try to pawn Rolexes to feed a drug habit."

"Oh no," Chloe cried.

John opened the second box. Amused, he grinned as he took out the watch. "Well, well, what do you know. Care to explain this, little lady?"

"I'm not a drug addict," Chloe said quickly. "Honestly."

John laughed. "I believe you, kid. I've known Nick long enough to know he wouldn't hang around with junkies." Taking his time, he examined both pieces carefully. "This isn't a knockoff," he finally said as he put the Rolex down next to the broach.

"You know me better than that," Nick declared. "I wouldn't try to con you."

"I know. So you want to pawn this stuff, huh?"

"That's the idea, yes," Nick said.

John stared at them for a long moment. "Are you two in some kind of trouble?"

"No," Nick protested hotly. "We just need some cash."

"Why don't you borrow it from your mom or your uncle Bobby?" John asked.

"Because we don't want them to know about it," Chloe blurted.

Nick shot her a quick frown. "What she means is we don't want anyone to know that we need cash because we've got something special in mind we want to do with it."

John cocked his head to one side. "I've known your family for over twenty years," he said. "Your dad was my best friend. If you're in some kind of trouble . . ."

"We're not in trouble," Chloe said. "We're trying to do a good deed. Honest."

"A good deed?"

"She's telling the truth," Nick put in. "We need some cash to do someone a good turn. So look, if I promise that we're not in any kind of trouble, can we pawn this stuff for cash?"

"How much you need?"

"Six hundred would do it," Nick said.

"You got it," John said. "But I'm not going to give you a claim check for this stuff—the six hundred is a loan, okay?"

Chloe looked at Nick. John Paradise was his friend, not hers. It had to be his decision.

Nick hesitated for a moment and then shrugged. "Okay, if that's the best we can do. But I don't know when we can pay you back."

"At least hang on to the pieces until we can pay you back," Chloe added.

"All right." John counted cash out of the register. "But I won't put them on display."

Chloe was mentally calculating how long it would take her to earn the six hundred bucks. If she used her clothing allowance and her regular allowance, got a part-time job and stopped getting her hair cut at Antonio's, she ought to be able to swing it in a couple of months. "I think we can pay you back by Thanksgiving," she said.

Nick shot her a strange look and put the bills away. "Thanks, John," he said. "We owe you one."

They said their good-byes and walked out. Chloe's stomach growled as they reached the car. "Thank goodness that's over," she said.

"Is that your stomach?" he asked as he unlocked the passenger door and pulled it open.

"Yeah, I didn't eat this morning." Chloe climbed in and leaned across to unlock the driver's side. "I was too nervous," she admitted.

"There's a restaurant over on Melrose that's okay," he said. "I could go for a burger myself."

Nick didn't talk again until they were sitting across from each other in a big, roomy back booth at Ondine's, a coffee shop that hadn't been redecorated since the swinging sixties. The Beatles wailed from loudspeakers on the walls, the scent of frying grease was strong enough to choke a horse, and the place was crowded with the kind of people that didn't live in suburbia.

Chloe examined her surroundings with interest. Along the crowded counter, a man with a black satin cape draped over his jeans and UCLA sweatshirt sat drinking coffee next to a perfectly groomed white-haired gentleman wearing a sporty blue blazer, pristine white shirt, and a paisley ascot. In the booth across from them, four punkers, all with pierced noses, eyebrows, and lips, argued loudly about global warming. The two elderly ladies in the booth next to the punkers ignored the loud argument. Their attention was focused exclusively on the tarot cards in front of them.

"This is a really interesting place," Chloe said as she turned and grinned at Nick. Her smile faded. He was staring at her closely, as though he was watching her for a reason. She suddenly realized she knew what he was up to. "But then you knew what it was like, didn't you? That's why you brought me here. You wanted to see if I'd freak."

Nick nodded slowly. "Yeah, I guess I did. I don't know, I guess this was a kind of test. I wanted to see how you would handle it."

"I think it's neat," she replied honestly. "Interesting. I understand why you thought I'd freak. Before the accident, I would have. I'd have been scared to death to be around people who were so different from me."

A blonde waitress brought them glasses of water and silverware setups. "You know what you want yet?"

"They have a burger special which is fabulous," Nick said.

"That's what I'll have."

"Make it two," Nick told the woman. As soon as she disappeared, he said to Chloe, "Look, I don't know what's going on with you and I'll be honest, I don't know if I even trust you, but I want you to know something.''

"What?" she asked with a bright smile. Now that she'd passed his dippy test, maybe he was beginning to like her a little. Chloe hated admitting, even to herself, how much it would mean to have Nick actually like her. But it meant a lot. She'd repressed the thought, but she'd always had a kind of crush on him.

He took a deep breath. "There's no way to be polite about this, so I'll just tell you straight out."

Chloe's bright smile faded. "Go ahead."

"Like I said, I don't know what you're up to. . . ."

"I'm not up to anything," she protested. "I'm trying to make things right."

He waved his hand impatiently. "So you say, but let's face it, you don't exactly have much of a track record for honesty."

"People can change."

"Sure they can," he agreed, "but usually something happens to make them change. Frankly, except for totaling that fancy car your old man bought you and getting a bump on the head, I can't see anything else that makes me think you've really changed on a deep, fundamental level. I know you claim you died for a couple of minutes, but as far as I'm concerned, that doesn't mean anything. What I'm trying to say is that if this is one of your cons and it blows up in my face and hurts me or my mom, I'll make you really sorry."

Stunned, Chloe simply stared at him. She'd thought he was beginning to trust her. She'd thought he sensed she wasn't the same person she used to be. But she was wrong. Nick was only going along with her because he wanted his mother to stay with her father. A little voice in the back of her mind warned her she'd be a fool to think he could ever grow to like her, even a little. As for any other fantasies she might have entertained about him, well, she could forget them, too.

"Don't worry," she finally said. "This isn't a con. I'm just trying to make up for all the nasty things I did to Lucinda."

Nick nodded and looked down at his hands.

A heavy silence, made even more obvious by the cheerful noise surrounding them, fell on them like a wet blanket. Chloe stared at the bright orange Formica tabletop. Maybe this was her real punishment . . . to do the best she could, to try and make up for all the rotten things she'd done, and to have no one ever, ever believe her.

Maybe it was what she deserved. But the moment that thought entered her head, she knew it was wrong. For crying out loud, she'd been a hateful, manipulative little brat, but she hadn't killed anyone. She wasn't a criminal. Her head jerked up and her eyes narrowed angrily. "Why is it so hard for you to understand that I've changed? I didn't just bump my head in that accident. I died."

"Yeah, and your old man's getting ready to sue the pants off someone because of it," Nick hissed. He sat back as the waitress brought their food.

As soon as the waitress disappeared, Chloe said, "That's not the point, you jerk." She was really angry now. "The point is that when I died, something happened. Long tunnel, bright light, overwhelming peace and love . . .''

''Oh yeah, you sound real full of peace and love right now,'' he taunted.

''I didn't say I've become a saint, I said I've changed,'' she shot back. Pissed off as she was, she was still hungry. She snatched up the ketchup bottle and dumped some on her fries. ''Dying does that to people, in case you haven't heard. I'm different now; my priorities have changed. I'm going to make up for every awful thing I've ever done to anyone so that when the time comes I can go with a clear conscience.''

Nick, who'd just picked up his burger, went completely still. ''What the hell are you talking about?'' he demanded.

''I'm talking about when it's over, when I've done what I was sent back to do,'' she muttered. Funny, she wasn't as ticked off as before. Now that she'd exploded she felt much better. Being a saint was hard on the nerves. All that repression. Just went to show that you could let off a little steam and still not be a horrible human being. She picked up the salt shaker and gave her fries a heavy dusting.

''Chloe.'' Nick put his food down. ''I want you to tell me exactly what you mean by that.''

Chloe popped a fry in her mouth. ''Umm, this is good. What do I mean? Well, exactly what I said. The next time I want to go with a clear conscience. Not that you particularly have to do that. I mean, it's not a prerequisite for the peace and love and stuff. But now that I know what's ahead, it would be nice to do it right this time.''

"I heard that part," he snapped. "Frankly, it gives me the creeps. What kind of sick fantasy are you into now?"

"You don't give up, do you?" She sighed. "Why am I even bothering? After that little lecture you just gave me, I don't have to tell you a thing. But just to show that I'm not a petty person anymore, I'll keep talking. This is not a sick fantasy. Get this through your thick head: I died. I went down the tunnel—bright lights, peace, love, et cetera . . .''

"I got that part," he interrupted. "I'm not sure I buy it, but I'm willing to give you the benefit of the doubt."

"A few minutes ago you were threatening me," she argued.

"I didn't mean it," he admitted grudgingly. "I was just trying to rattle you so that if you were up to one of your schemes you'd back off. But what's all this crap about 'the next time' and 'clear conscience'? You're not planning on doing something stupid, are you?"

It took a moment for her to understand what he was talking about. "You mean am I going to kill myself?" She couldn't help it—she laughed.

He glared at her. "I don't see what's so funny. The way you've been talking is pretty weird."

"Not to me," she said, shrugging. "It's perfectly natural. But facts are facts. I was sent back for a reason."

"We're all here for a reason," he replied.

"Of course," she agreed. She took a huge bite of her burger. "This is really good," she mumbled around the mouthful of food. "But my reason is fairly specific. Otherwise, I'd be dead. I mean, I wouldn't have come back unless there was something specific I had to do. Kinda neat actually, because I get a shot at making up for all the horrible stuff I did, too. I just hope I've got enough time left. I mean, it's impossible to know why I was sent back. It might be something real dramatic like pulling someone out of a raging river or it might seem to be real boring."

Nick shook his head in amazement. "I don't believe this."

"You seem to have a problem with that," she replied. "But take my word for it, it's true." She popped another fry in her mouth. She couldn't believe how good food tasted.

"I'm not saying I don't believe you," he said. "I'm saying I don't believe this whole situation. But look, Chloe, you're heading into muddy waters here. Have you ever heard of a 'self-fulfilling prophecy'?"

"Kinda," she muttered. "Is that like where you say you're going to have a lousy time visiting your relatives and then you go and because you've set yourself up to be miserable, you are?"

"That's it," he said. He hadn't touched his own food. "I think that's what you're doing. I don't know what really happened to you, but if you think you're going to kick off after you've atoned for all the supposedly bad things you've done . . ."

"That's not it," she insisted. "I'm not going to die until after I've done what I was sent back to do. Atoning for being a lousy person is sort of a side issue. Kinda like a side effect. Are you going to eat those fries?''

''Help yourself.'' He shoved his plate toward her. ''Okay, even if what you say is true and you're not going to go until you've done whatever it is you think you've got to do, you could still be setting yourself up.'' He finally reached for his burger and took a bite. But he didn't look like he enjoyed it much.

''Don't worry.'' Chloe polished off the last of her sandwich. ''I'm not setting myself up. Anyway, are we going to Jason and Tina's after we eat? We need to give them the money.''

Nick put his food down. ''I'll go give them a call. Since they're not working, they ought to be home.''

''Aren't you going to finish your burger?''

''Nah, I've lost my appetite.''

The condo was located up in the hills. It was the corner unit of a complex done in pale orange-beige stucco, and was beautifully landscaped to blend perfectly with the wild setting of the hillside. Small grass verges ran along the sides and front of the buildings, flower beds filled with bright yellow and pink blossoms were visible in the common areas, and there was plenty of guest parking. Through a grove of trees below the parking lot she could see the inviting blue of a large swimming pool.

''Wow,'' Chloe said as they got out of the car. ''The view alone must be worth a fortune.'' Even with the layer of L.A. smog blanketing the valley, you could see for miles and miles.

"It's better at night when you can see the lights," Nick said. He started for the unit closest to them, walked up the short walkway, and rang the doorbell.

Chloe caught up with him just as the door opened and a beautiful blonde-haired woman, probably in her late forties, stuck her head out. "Hi, Nick," she exclaimed. "It was such a nice surprise when you called. Come on in." She held the door wide open and waved them inside.

"Hi, Tina," Nick replied as he and Chloe stepped across the threshold. "I hope you don't mind our dropping by like this. This is my, uh, stepsister, Chloe Marlowe. Chloe, this is Tina Everett; her working handle is Tina Eldridge."

Chloe extended her hand. "I'm very pleased to meet you," she said. "I've seen you on television. But you're even prettier in real life." Up close, Tina was gorgeous. Her skin was flawless, her cheekbones perfect, and her eyes a warm, smiling brown.

"Why thank you," Tina said. "Come in and sit down," she invited, leading them into a living room with high cathedral ceilings and a fireplace at the far end. Chloe looked around with interest as she followed her hostess toward a pale green leather sofa. The walls were covered with framed movie posters, signed pictures of famous actors, and what looked like Tina in a medieval period costume.

Tina gestured at the couch. "Have a seat, I'll go get Jason. I'm sure he'd like to see you."

Chloe plopped down and glanced at the copies of *Variety, Dramalogue,* and *The Hollywood Reporter* strewn haphazardly across the glass coffee table. On the end table next to the love seat across from her there was a silver framed photograph of Tina and Lucinda with a much younger Nick sitting between them. Next to that was a photo of Lucinda, a man, and a ten-year-old Nick without his two front teeth.

She started when Nick sat down next to her. "You photograph nicely," she said, pointing toward the table.

He laughed. "Jason's an amateur photographer. He and my dad were always taking pictures. That's my dad there next to Mom."

Chloe smiled. "You look like him."

"Hey, hey, fella," a male voice cut into the quiet room. "What brings you down this way?"

Nick, a huge grin on his face, got to his feet. "Hi, Jason, how's it going?"

Chloe found herself staring at one of the handsomest men she'd ever laid eyes on. His hair was dark brown and brushed straight back from a high forehead. His mouth was wide and generous, his chin strong and manly, and his cheekbones could have been chiseled from stone.

"Who's your friend?" he asked, giving her a friendly grin when he saw her gaping at him.

"This is my stepsister, Chloe." Nick popped back down as Jason took a seat on the far side of the couch. Tina, who'd come in right behind him, sat down next to her husband.

"Your stepsister?" Jason's perfect eyebrows rose in surprise. "I didn't think the two of you got along."

"We've become friends," Nick said quickly. He

reached over to pat her arm. "Chloe isn't so bad once you get to know her."

"Gee, thanks," she muttered.

"Can I get you something to drink?" Tina asked. "We've got iced tea in the fridge. Or a soft drink?"

"No, that's okay," Nick answered for both of them. "We just ate. We're not going to stay long. Actually, we've got kind of a funny reason for dropping by."

"Shoot," Jason said easily. But he and his wife exchanged a puzzled glance.

"Well." Nick cleared his throat. "I don't know what Mom has told you about her situation."

"Only that she and Chloe's father are separating," Tina said. "She's planning on moving in here next week. But if she needs to come earlier, Jason and I can move out right away. We're going to stay up at the cabin in Big Bear."

"But isn't that kind of a long ways to commute when you're looking for work?" Nick asked.

Jason laughed. "We've done it before. We're actors, kid. It's either feast or famine with us."

"Thank God we had the good sense to buy the place when I had that part on *Days*," Tina said earnestly. "It'll be a pain to commute that distance, but I don't think it'll be for long. I've got a second read for a part on a sitcom filming over at Fox and Jason's got a callback for a dog food commercial."

"But it would be easier if you could stay here for a little while, wouldn't it?" Nick pressed.

"Sure," Jason said. "But we're not freeloaders.

Even though I know your mother wouldn't kick us out, it's best if we go up to the cabin.''

"But if you had the rent, you'd stay?" Nick persisted.

Jason frowned in confusion. "Not really. Your mom wants to move in here, and it is her condo.''

"She only wants to move in here because of me," Chloe blurted. "And Nick and I are trying to make her see that she loves my dad and he loves her. They don't really want to split up.''

"Kids," Tina said softly, "I'm not sure what you're getting at here, but we don't have any right to interfere in Lucinda's personal life.''

"We're not asking you to interfere," Chloe said with conviction. "We're the ones doing that. But it's for a good cause. They're only splitting up because of me. Because I was such a witch. But I know they love each other.''

"Look," Jason interrupted. "Whatever reasons you kids have for coming here are pretty irrelevant. We won't take advantage of our friendship with Lucinda. The bottom line is, we can't pay the rent.''

"Oh yes you can," Nick said firmly. "We'll loan you the money.''

CHAPTER
SIX

"Whew," Chloe commented as Nick pulled away from the parking lot. "That was one tough sell. I was beginning to get worried that they weren't going to go for it."

"Yeah, me too," Nick muttered. "Let's hope that Mom doesn't blow a gasket when they call and tell her they need the place for another month."

"Your mom's not likely to do that," Chloe said quickly. "I mean, she's generally pretty cool about things. Especially if they keep to that story about the cabin windows being busted out by vandals and their not having the cash to get them fixed yet."

Nick shook his head. "I don't know, Chloe. This is starting to feel funny. Maybe we shouldn't be interfering like this."

"They wouldn't be getting a divorce if *I* hadn't interfered in the first place," Chloe argued. "But I'll understand if you want to bow out of this. If it blows up in our faces, I'll take the heat for it, honest. I'll make sure your mom doesn't blame you."

Nick shot her a fast, irritated look. "That's not what I'm worried about. I'm a big boy—I don't need you covering for me. It just doesn't feel right, sticking my nose in other people's business. And I didn't like putting Tina and Jason on the spot like that, either."

"I don't much like the feeling either," she admitted glumly. "To be honest, I can't understand how I could have done it so much BD."

"BD?"

"Before Dying," she mumbled absently.

"Damn, that's morbid," he snapped.

"It is not," she shot back. "It's efficient. Whether you believe me or not, I feel like a different person now. Dividing my life into two parts seems to make sense."

"I'm not going to have this conversation with you," he gritted out. "It's too bizarre. Now, I suggest we decide how we're going to handle the next step."

Chloe frowned at him. What was wrong? Nick hadn't ever struck her as the sensitive type before. Why should he care that she was so casual about what had happened? After all, it wasn't as if he was the one who'd pegged out. But there wasn't much point in arguing with him. "Are you sure you want there to be a next step? I don't want you going along with this if your doubts are going to bug your conscience."

"Don't worry, I'll get over it." He shrugged and flipped on the turn signal indicator. "Like you said, our interfering is for a good cause. But we'd better make sure we do this right."

"What do you mean?"

"Mom's going to expect some kind of reaction

when she announces she isn't moving," he said. "How good an actress are you? Can you look surprised?"

"I think so," she replied. She glanced at the traffic out the window. They were heading down Sunset toward the 101 Freeway.

"You think so?" Nick challenged. "You'll have to do better than that. Mom's no fool. I don't want her suspecting that something is up when Tina calls."

"I can act surprised," she assured him. "What else?"

He thought for a moment. "This is getting complicated. Where did you tell your dad we were going today?"

"Nowhere," she replied. "I mean, I didn't say anything to anyone. Your mom was out and gone when I got up and my dad was on the phone. So I just took off."

"Okay." Nick slowed the car and pulled into the lane leading to the on-ramp. "Where are you going to tell them you were today? We'd better get our stories straight."

Chloe was prepared for that one. "Shopping. I'm going to tell Dad that I bribed you into taking me to the Sherman Oaks Galleria. Since I totaled my car, he'll believe me."

"I'm not sure my mom will," Nick muttered. He said nothing as he concentrated on getting them on the freeway. As soon as they were cruising safely north, he said, "Mom knows you're not my favorite person."

"Tell her I paid you to take me," Chloe suggested. "She'll believe that."

Nick shot her another strange look. "Naw, I'll just tell her that I'm willing to give you another chance."

Chloe said nothing. For a moment, she found herself wishing that what he said was true. That he really was willing to give her another chance. But it wasn't the truth. Nick had his own reasons for helping, and she knew she'd better remember that.

Three days later, Chloe was ready to scream. She cornered Nick in front of the refrigerator. "How come we haven't heard from Tina and Jason?" she asked in a low voice. Lucinda and Dan were in the dining room. Carlotta had gone to her sister's for the weekend and Chloe, making good on her promise, was getting dinner ready.

"I don't know," Nick hissed. "They should have called by now." He broke off and sniffed. "Is something burning?"

"Oh no!" Chloe whirled around, grabbed a pot holder, and yanked open the oven. "My dinner rolls!" She pulled them out and sighed in relief. "They're not too bad, just a little brown."

"What else are we having?" Nick asked eagerly.

"Rib roast"—she nodded toward a foil-covered mound sitting on the counter—"roast spuds, steamed carrots, and salad."

"Wow, that's pretty fancy." He sounded impressed.

"Actually," Chloe admitted, "it sounds a lot fancier than it is. Besides, I can't take credit for it. Carlotta did most of the work before she left. She gave me detailed instructions so I wouldn't screw up.''

''Hey, Chloe,'' her father's voice came from the dining room. ''When are we going to eat? I'm starving.''

''It's coming now,'' she called.

''I'll give you a hand,'' Nick volunteered. He opened the fridge and got out the salad. ''If we don't hear from Tina and Jason by tomorrow, I'll give them a call,'' he whispered as he headed for the dining room.

Chloe nodded and dumped the rolls in the basket she had waiting. When Nick came back, she handed it to him. ''I'll bring the roast if you'll take this.''

It didn't take long to get the rest of the food onto the table. She felt pretty proud as she sat the rib roast in front of her father to be carved.

''This looks really good,'' Dan said as he picked up the carving set. ''You weren't kidding. You can cook.''

''Carlotta helped me,'' Chloe said. ''And even if she hadn't, this is pretty simple.''

''It looks lovely,'' Lucinda said. She gave Chloe a genuine smile.

Dan began carving the meat. ''I spoke to Jack King today. He's the attorney for the county.''

''You're still not thinking of suing those paramedics, are you?'' Chloe wailed. She'd hoped her father had given that up.

''Well . . .'' Dan slapped a large piece of meat onto a plate and handed it to Lucinda. ''That remains to be seen. I will admit, I've had second thoughts about it, especially as you don't seem to be suffering any ill effects.''

"I'm not, Dad," Chloe said quickly. "Honestly, I've never felt better in my life. Please don't sue them. They did everything they could for me that night."

"Honey, you don't know that," Dan cautioned. "You were unconscious."

"But I—" She broke off as Nick gave her a sharp kick under the table. She caught his warning look and quickly clamped her mouth shut. Though for the life of her she couldn't figure out what he was up to. She was only going to tell her father the truth. That she could remember everything that had happened that night. That she'd seen it clearly from her vantage point of floating outside her body.

"You what?" Dan asked, handing her a plate.

"I'm glad you changed your mind," she said. "Thanks, Dad. It means a lot to me."

"I'm only doing it for you," he said gruffly. "Like Nick said, putting you through the trauma of a trial wouldn't do your nervous system any good."

She glanced at Nick, but he was dumping roast potatoes and carrots onto his plate and wouldn't meet her eye.

"This is very good," Lucinda said softly. "You did okay. As a matter of fact, you've worked really hard lately. I saw you carrying Mrs. Cardell's groceries in for her. That was really nice of you."

Chloe was warmed by her praise. She'd worked hard the past three days to atone for being such a brat. She'd helped Carlotta do the housework and laundry, ran errands, and carried in their neighbors' groceries, and even tried to assist Mr. Loggins, their gardener. After she'd trampled his cuttings for the third time, though, he'd told her to please go away. But she was glad that someone had noticed she was at least trying. "Thanks. Mrs. Cardell's a nice lady. I know it's hard for her to get around with that walker of hers, and I don't mind helping. Those heavy groceries are too hard for her to handle on her own."

Nick cleared his throat. "Uh, Mom, have you heard from Tina or Jason lately? Have they moved out yet?"

Lucinda grinned. "Tina called me a couple of days ago. She and Jason will need a few more days to get moved out." Her smile vanished as she realized that Dan was looking at her expectantly. "I hope you don't mind if I'm here a bit longer?" she asked.

Dan shook his head quickly. "No, not at all. Take your time."

"Thanks. I didn't think you'd care, but I guess I should have told you earlier."

"It's no problem," Dan said. "You can stay as long as you need. We . . . uh, may be divorcing, but we can be civilized to one another."

Chloe pretended to be interested in her food, but she was listening carefully. Jeez, it was as obvious as the nose on your face. These two were still crazy in love with each other. They were falling all over themselves to find reasons to stay together. Smug in the knowledge that thanks to her and Nick they soon wouldn't have to find excuses, Chloe popped a bit of rib roast into her mouth.

"Why do they need more time?" Nick asked.

"Oh, you know Tina and Jason. They got a wad of cash a couple of days ago and instead of doing something sensible, they took off for Vegas."

Chloe choked.

Chloe didn't get a chance to talk to Nick alone until later that night. Dan and Lucinda had insisted on helping clear up and load the dishwasher.

She paused outside of Nick's room. Through the door, she could hear the Mighty Mighty Bosstones wailing softly. Checking once again to make sure the coast was clear, she knocked softly.

"What took you so long?" Nick whispered as he pulled the door open and yanked her inside. "We've got a crisis here, you know."

"What took me so long?" she repeated indignantly. "I had to clean up and what's more, my dad and your mom decided to help. No offense meant, but things might have gone a bit smoother if you'd hung around to run interference."

"Why?" Nick's expression was concerned. "Were they fighting?"

"Worse—they danced around each other so politely it took ages to get anything done." She sank down on Nick's bed. She noticed he'd picked up a little. Either that or he'd just shoved all his dirty laundry in the closet and slammed the door shut. "Where did you disappear to?"

"I came up here," he replied, sinking down on the bed next to her. "I've been trying to get ahold of Tina or Jason and ask them what in the world's going on. But all I got was their answering machine."

"Great," she muttered. "Do you think this means they took our cash to gamble with?"

"I don't think they had any of their own," he said. He got to his feet and began pacing the small room. "This is all my fault."

"Your fault?" Chloe couldn't help it—she had to laugh. "You've got to be kidding. Why is it your fault? It was my idea to give them the money. Besides, do we know for sure they've taken our cash? Maybe they had this trip to Vegas planned for a long time and they'll pay the rent when they get back? I mean, I don't think we ought to be jumping to any conclusions here."

"They were broke, Chloe," Nick said wearily. "People who don't have rent money don't plan trips to Vegas. Face it, we've been had."

"I don't believe it," she insisted. "They're friends of your mom's."

"They're flaky actors."

"They weren't going to freeload off your mom," she pointed out, recalling how they'd had to talk themselves blue in the face to get the Everetts to take their cash.

Nick stopped pacing and looked at her. "Yeah, that's true. I guess I just panicked there for a while. There's got to be a reasonable explanation."

"There is," she assured him. Chloe had decided it was much better to go through life believing the best of people; she had firsthand knowledge of what it felt like to have people think the worst of you. "Trust me. They'll come through."

"Let's hope they do it quick. This morning Mom

asked me to keep next Friday open so I could help her move.'' Nick ran his fingers through his hair. ''So Tina and Jason had better have that rent to her by the first of the week.''

''They will.'' Chloe got to her feet and started for the door.

''Uh, just a minute.''

She turned to look at him. ''What?''

''Are you busy now?'' he asked casually. ''I mean, it's Friday night. I'm kinda tired of being cooped up in here. You want to go get an ice cream or something?''

She was so surprised she didn't say anything for a minute.

''It's okay if you don't want to,'' he said quickly.

''No, no,'' she hurried to reassure him. ''I'd love to get out for a few minutes. I'm just surprised that you asked, that's all.''

He grinned. ''Yeah, well, you're not as bad as you used to be.''

''Gee, thanks,'' she retorted. But she was thrilled that Nick was finally starting to like her. Even if it was just a little. She reached for the door handle. ''Let me go get my purse.''

''I'll meet you downstairs,'' he called as she left. ''Oh, Chloe.''

Again, she stopped and turned.

''Be sure and tell your dad we're going out,'' he instructed.

Chloe's high spirits began to sag. She had a feeling she knew what was coming. ''Why?''

''Because if your dad thinks you and I are going

out together, he'll start talking to my mom, get it?"
He smiled broadly, obviously pleased with himself for
coming up with the idea on the spur of the moment.
"I mean, if we want these two to stay together, we've
got to get them talking about something other than
how good the roast potatoes are."

With an effort, she kept the smile on her lips. But
she was crushed. Nick wasn't interested in getting to
know her better, nor was he beginning to like her. He
was simply doing his best to come up with ways to
keep their parents' marriage together. "Yeah, I guess
you're right."

She hurried to her room. She hated admitting to
herself that she was so shallow, but the truth was, she
was disappointed. She'd allowed herself to believe
that since their trip to L.A. together, they'd gotten
closer. She'd really, really hoped he was beginning to
like her. Maybe even as more than just a stepsister.
Disgusted with herself for indulging in such stupid
fantasies, Chloe grabbed her purse and started for the
door. Hoping that Nick would ever see her as anything except an obnoxious stepsister was stupid, so
she might as well do a little more atoning tonight.

"That was fast," he said as she came down the
stairs. "It usually takes you forever to get ready to
go out."

She sighed in frustration and glanced down at her
old denim shorts and tank top. Hadn't anyone noticed
she'd changed? It used to be she wouldn't set foot out
of the house unless her makeup was on, her hair was
perfect, and she was dressed to kill.

"All I had to do was grab my purse," she replied.

In the living room, she could see her father and Lucinda staring at them curiously. "Is it okay with you if we go get some ice cream?" she called.

"I've already told them," Nick said.

"It's fine," her father yelled. "Just be careful. It's a Friday night so there's a lot of traffic coming into town from L.A."

The air felt warm as they stepped out of the air-conditioned house and into the night. "It must be tough not having wheels," Nick commented as they walked toward the curb to his car.

"It's not so bad," Chloe said. "You get used to it. Besides, it's kind of nice taking the bus. Not as convenient as driving, but interesting."

"You took the bus?" Nick asked incredulously as he walked around to the driver's side.

"Sure." Chloe slid into the front seat. "Mrs. Cardell doesn't have a car. That's how we got to the grocery store and back—we went on the bus. How'd you think we got there?"

Nick shot her another one of those weird, unreadable glances and then shoved the key in the ignition. "I didn't realize you'd gone with her; I thought you were just helping her carry those bags into her house."

"Naw, we were on the bus," Chloe confided. "Besides, if she drives a car the way she handles a grocery cart, I can see why they took her license away. Don't get in that old lady's way—I mean, she's ruthless. Hey, do you mind if we swing around and pick up Mia? She was stuck home tonight." Chloe didn't add that Mia was generally stuck home every Friday night.

"She'd probably jump at the chance to get out for a while."

Nick shrugged. "Sure, we can go get her." He angled a fast glance in her direction as he pulled up to a stoplight. "I just didn't think you really liked her all that much."

"Meaning you think I used to just use her?"

"I didn't say that," he shot back.

"Don't worry, I wasn't trying to be nasty." Chloe sighed. Whoever said confession was good for the soul obviously didn't have as much to confess as she did. "I'm the first to admit I used to take advantage of Mia. But not anymore. She's too good a person for that. She's honest and kind and very, very smart. I'm lucky she was willing to give me a second chance. She lives on Durant Street; that's right off Twin Oaks Boulevard."

"I know where it is," he told her. He reached over and turned on the radio. Chloe rolled down her window and took a deep breath. She was suddenly filled with an unexplainable sensation of joy. The scent of the summer night filled her nostrils; she looked up and saw a few bright stars twinkling overhead and was awed by the simple beauty she'd always taken for granted. They turned onto Twin Oaks and she realized that the tawdry neon signs and the shapes of the huge trees enveloping the street had their own mysterious kind of loveliness. Chloe sighed deeply. It was so good to be alive.

"Hey, Earth to Chloe," Nick yelled.

"Oh, sorry, I was dreaming," she apologized. "What?"

"Which one is it?" He nodded at the row of apartments ahead of them. Chloe realized they'd turned onto Mia's street.

"It's the second one from the corner down there." She pointed toward the end of the small road.

Nick pulled up at the curb and Chloe climbed out. "I'll be right back."

She hurried across the small front yard and up the stairs of the two-story building. Mia lived in the first apartment at the top. Chloe rang the bell and waited.

"Who is it?" Mia's voice came from the other side of the closed door.

"It's Chloe. Nick and I are— Hi," she broke off as the door flew open and Mia's head popped out.

"Hi, yourself. What are you doing here?" Mia was grinning from ear to ear.

"Who's there, honey?" Mia's mom called from the living room.

"It's Chloe."

"Hi, Mrs. Coleridge," Chloe called.

"Hi, Chloe."

"We're going out for ice cream and we wondered if you wanted to come with us," she said to Mia.

Mia looked stunned for a moment and then grinned. "I'd love to. Uh, who's 'we'?"

"Me and Nick."

Mia's eyebrows rose in surprise for a split second before she caught herself. "Great. I'd love to come. Let me grab my purse." Leaving the door cracked open, she disappeared only to reappear a moment later with a small purse slung over her shoulder. "I'll be back in a little while," she called to her mom.

"Since when did you and Nick become such close friends?" Mia asked as they climbed down the stairs and headed for the car.

"Since we started trying to get Lucinda and my dad to patch up their differences," Chloe said softly. "Look, it's only an ice cream, not a hot date. We're not exactly best friends."

Chloe slid back into the front seat and Mia got in the back. "Hi," she said to Nick.

"Hi." Nick looked over his shoulder and gave her a big smile. "Glad you could make it."

"I'm the one who's glad," Mia gushed. "It's nice getting out of that apartment. It's so hot."

Chloe cringed guiltily. Mia's place wasn't air-conditioned. She should have thought of that and invited her over for the night. "Would you like to spend the night at my house?" she asked quickly. "It's a little cooler."

"Nah," she replied, "I don't like leaving Mom alone at night. But thanks for asking."

"You want to drive over to the coast? There's some cool places in Santa Barbara. You know, bookstores and funky ice cream parlors." Nick tilted his head slightly, making sure that he was talking to Mia as much as he was to Chloe.

"I'd like that," Mia said hesitantly. "But only if the two of you are sure it's okay."

"How about it, Chloe?" Nick asked eagerly.

"That would be wonderful," she replied.

"Great. Let's go. So what have you been doing this summer, Mia?" he asked.

"Nothing much, just hanging out and working

whenever I could," she replied. She leaned up against the front seat, which put her almost directly between them. "I don't have a real job, just baby-sitting and stuff like that."

"Baby-sitting sounds like a real job to me." Nick gave her a warm smile.

"I'm kinda looking forward to school starting," Mia continued shyly.

"Me, too." Nick flashed her another fast grin. "Not that I'm looking forward to spending my weekends cracking the books, but doing nothing but working gets boring."

Mia laughed.

Chloe wondered what was so darned funny. In the darkened car there was just enough light from the overhead streetlamps and the dash for her to see Mia. Her friend was staring at Nick with a dopey, awestruck expression on her face. Jeez, Chloe thought, you'd think the girl had never seen a good-looking guy before. Then she was immediately ashamed of herself. Mia was her friend, for goodness' sake. So what if she had a little crush on Nick? He could be a pretty cool person when he wanted to. He was being really, really nice to Mia. But then again, why shouldn't he? Mia was nice, sweet, and pretty.

Chloe felt a sudden, sick emptiness in the pit of her stomach. In a flash she recognized the emotion as jealousy. Shame, hot and ugly, ripped through her, leaving her shaken and feeling angry. Not at Mia—that would be dumb. But at herself for being so self-centered as to begrudge her friend a harmless flirtation.

What was wrong with her? Hadn't that trip down the tunnel shown her anything? Had she really changed?

"Earth to Chloe." Nick's voice jerked her out of her thoughts.

"What?" Her tone was sharper than she intended and she winced at the look Nick gave her. "I mean, I'm sorry, I was kinda dreaming again. What did you say?"

"I said, do you want to go to the pier when we get there?" he asked. "It's still pretty early. There's always something going on there. The people-watching alone is usually better than the movies. Mia's game. Is there a reason for you and me to get back?"

Chloe shrugged nonchalantly. "Not that I know of. Sure, we can go on the pier. It ought to be really spectacular tonight. The view, I mean. There's a crescent moon out. . . ." She paused as she suddenly realized there was a way to prove to herself that she'd really changed.

That she wasn't the same self-centered brat she'd always been.

"As a matter of fact, why don't the two of you hit the pier," she said quickly, "while I check out a bookstore. There's a couple of things I want to look up."

"You don't want to come with us?" Mia asked timidly. "Are you sure?"

Chloe took a deep breath. There was nothing that she'd rather have done than walk on the pier in the moonlight with Nick. But Nick didn't like her. From the way he was acting, he was interested in Mia.

The only decent thing to do was to give them a chance to get to know each other.

"Absolutely," she stated. She was going to do the right thing. She was going to give her friend a chance to get to know Nick.

No matter how much it hurt.

CHAPTER
SEVEN

They parked in a public lot near State Street and walked over to the end of the pier. The streets were crowded with tourists, student types, and locals out for the evening. Chloe, who'd deliberately gone on ahead to give Mia and Nick a chance to walk together, dodged around an elderly couple walking a cocker spaniel and then scooted out of the way of the milling crowds. She leaned up against the edge of a building and waited for Nick and Mia to catch up. They weren't far behind, but they were walking slowly, with their heads close together as they talked. They were enjoying their conversation, she thought, judging by the expression on Mia's face.

Another pang hit her, but this time it wasn't jealousy. It was something else, something that made her want to smile and cry at the same time. Smile because she was alive on a summer night with two people she'd come to care deeply about and cry because the moment was so fleeting. Like one of those melodramatic, blockbuster movies that everyone sneered at but bawled their eyes out over. That's how she felt, like she was starring in her very own melodrama and only she knew for sure what the ending was going to be.

"What's with you, ashamed to be seen with us?" Nick's tone was teasing, but Chloe sensed that beneath the banter he was serious.

"Of course not," she protested. "There wasn't enough room for all of us to walk together. You know how I hate being crowded."

"There's an ice cream place right there," Mia said, pointing up the street.

"Why don't we meet there in an hour," Chloe said quickly. Much as it hurt, she was determined to give Mia some private time with Nick. "Is that okay?"

Nick nodded and without another word, turned and punched the button on the streetlight. Mia grinned happily as Chloe, with a shrug of her shoulders, turned in the opposite direction and made her way up the street.

What was wrong with Nick now? She was just trying to give him a chance. She'd finally figured out that between his school schedule and working on his uncle's ranch, Nick didn't have a lot of time to meet girls. He'd moved up here from L.A. when his mom married her dad. She'd only now realized that one of the reasons he'd been so down on her all the time was because of his own loneliness. He was a great-looking guy and he had a terrific personality. It must have been tough on him to find himself living in a strange house in a new place and with none of his old friends around. She winced as she thought of all the times she could have invited him out with her and her crowd and hadn't.

Put that on the old atonement list, she told herself. Maybe by being generous tonight, by giving him and Mia a chance to be together, she was in some small way making up for having been such a selfish cow.

Even with the crowds, it took her less than ten minutes to get to the bookstore. It was one of the big chain stores that sold CDs and videos, and boasted a built-in coffeehouse, as well as selling books.

Chloe stepped through the heavy glass doors and took a deep breath, appreciating the luscious scent of freshly brewed java. She stood there for a moment, wondering what to go look at first. Since her accident, she'd discovered an almost insatiable appetite for reading. Before that, the only things she ever read were fashion magazines.

"Ohhh . . ." she yelped as she was jostled from behind. She stumbled and quickly caught herself before she slammed into a display of science fiction books.

"Oops . . . sorry about that," an apologetic male voice said. "Are you okay?"

She turned and came face-to-face with a guy who looked to be about eighteen. He had light brown hair, wire-rimmed glasses, and an embarrassed smile. "I'm really sorry," he continued when she didn't say anything. "Sometimes I just don't watch where I'm going."

"That's okay." She returned his smile. "It was my fault. I shouldn't have been standing here gawking.

But it always takes me a few minutes to make up my mind where I want to go first.''

He laughed. ''I thought I was the only one with that problem. Every time I come in here I can never decide whether to hit the mystery section or science fiction. There's always something in both that I want. What do you like to read?''

''I'm not sure,'' she replied honestly. Great, now he thought she was a dingbat.

Behind the frames of his glasses, his eyes widened. She noticed they were quite nice eyes. Big and blue and just about the same shade as the T-shirt he wore. ''You don't know what you like to read?''

It was Chloe's turn to laugh now. ''I know that sounds crazy,'' she said, ''but I've only recently discovered how much fun books can be. Actually, I thought I'd have a look in the religion section.'' She wasn't sure what compelled her to say that. The words seemed to pop out of her mouth of their own accord.

''It's downstairs,'' he said, pointing toward a staircase at the far end of the store.

''You work here?''

''No.'' He shook his head. ''I'm a Religious Studies major. I know where the religion section is in every bookstore between here and West L.A.''

''Religious Studies?'' Chloe couldn't believe her luck. ''You mean you're studying to be a minister?''

''Not exactly,'' he admitted. ''I haven't made up my mind about that yet. I'm not sure I've got the calling. Let's just say that what people believe fascinates me.''

She didn't hesitate. Maybe now she could find

some answers. Mia's help was all well and good; Chloe really appreciated her friend's assistance. But it wasn't every day that you ran into an expert, or at least the closest thing to an expert that she was likely to find. "My name's Chloe Marlowe," she said, extending her hand.

He was taken aback, but he recovered quickly and shook her hand. "Pleased to meet you. I'm Jed Robbins."

"Uh, if you've got a few minutes," she said, "I'd like to buy you a cup of coffee."

Chloe had to run to get to the ice cream parlor in time. She careened in through the open doors and skidded to a halt. Nick and Mia were already there, seated at one of the round glass tables and licking strawberry ice cream cones. Nick's was a double.

"Hey, what took you so long?" Nick called as he spotted her.

"Wait'll you hear," she said. "Let me get one of those and I'll be right over." She ordered a double chocolate cone and then hurried over and flopped down next to Mia.

"Hi," Mia said with a grin. Her cheeks were flushed, her eyes sparkled, and her hair was nicely tangled from the wind off the pier. All in all, she looked prettier than Chloe had ever seen her. "What's up?"

"I had the greatest stroke of luck." Chloe's tongue flicked out as she swiped at her cone. "I met this guy at the bookstore."

"What guy?" Nick asked. "What do you mean, 'you met him'? Met him how?"

"He accidentally bumped into me." The ice cream tasted so fabulous she took another quick lick. "But the important thing is, Jed's a Religious Studies major. I bought him a cup of coffee—"

"You picked him up?" Nick yelped.

"Of course not," she said defensively. "I introduced myself first. Besides, we were at a bookstore, not a club. That's hardly a pickup."

"The hell it's not. You didn't give him your phone number, did you?" Nick asked with a scowl.

"Well, yeah, kind of," Chloe admitted. "But not because he was interested in me or anything like that. Only because he's going to help me. I told him what happened to me . . . about the accident . . . about dying. I told him how confused I was and how it had really changed my life. Jed said there was all kinds of evidence that my experience was real. He's going to call me tomorrow with more information."

"Oh Chloe, that's great," Mia said enthusiastically.

"What's so great about it?" Nick muttered. "You were in a bookstore. Why didn't he just show you the books you needed?"

"He did," Chloe retorted. "He showed me a bunch of books on the subject. You'd be surprised at how common my experience is. . . ."

"Yeah, and lots of people claim they've been abducted by aliens, too," Nick said. "If this guy thinks these books are so great, why didn't he have you buy one? Why did he want your phone number?"

"He suggested I should buy them, but I only had

two bucks with me," she said. "Besides, a lot of information about the subject is in magazine articles, not books. Why are you being so negative about this? . . . Oh yeah, that's right, you think I've been lying about the whole thing anyway."

"I don't think that," he protested.

"That's not what you said before," she reminded him.

"Hey, guys," Mia interrupted. "Let's not argue. It's been a really neat evening. Let's not spoil it, okay?"

Nick looked at Mia and gave her a tight smile. Then he reached over and patted her hand. "Yeah, you're right. Why spoil a nice evening. Besides, it's none of my business who Chloe gives her phone number to."

Chloe was unbelievably hurt and she couldn't understand why. But one thing was for sure: She was going to keep her mouth shut from now on about her near death experience.

"Okay, we'll call a truce." She gave Mia a reassuring smile. But as they finished their ice cream and made their way back to the parking lot, Chloe couldn't help wondering why Nick was so upset. Did he hate her so much that he couldn't stand the thought she'd changed and might need a little spiritual guidance? Or did he just plain think she wasn't worth anyone's time or trouble?

Chloe woke suddenly. She turned her head and stared at the face of her clock radio. It was just past five and she was wide awake. Since the accident, she didn't seem to need nearly as much sleep. She threw the covers off and yawned. Might as well go downstairs and get some juice, she thought.

She moved quietly through the silent house. As she came close to the study, where her father was bunking, she rose on her tiptoes, not wanting a creaking floorboard to wake him from his much needed rest.

The study door was open a few inches, and Chloe stopped and reached for the handle, intending to quietly shut the door. Her gaze flicked into the room, toward the sleeper sofa. She went still. Her father wasn't there. Curious, she pushed the door open farther and stuck her head inside. The study was empty.

She was suddenly uneasy. The house had been quiet and dark when she and Nick had gotten home last night. "Oh no," she murmured, trying to fight off panic. What if her father and Lucinda had had a lulu of a fight and he'd done something dumb, like move out?

Turning, she flew down the hall to the living room. She peeked in. Nothing. He wasn't sacked out on the oversized sofa. Her spirits sank as she dashed up the stairs. She didn't think he'd gone to the guest room—he hated the mattress on that bed. She'd heard him complain about it after he'd slept there once when Lucinda was contagious with the flu. Her heart raced as she grabbed the doorknob and shoved into the guest room.

The bed was empty.

"Damn," she muttered. She bit her lip, wondering what to do now. This was a disaster. An absolute disaster. Tina and Jason taking off for Vegas was bad enough, but if her dad had left, that was even worse.

Slowly, she backed out of the room and straight into someone. Chloe yelped and whirled around.

"Shhhh, you'll wake up the whole house." Nick held his fingers to his lips. "What in the world are you doing."

"Looking for my father," she whispered. "What are you doing up this early?"

Nick yawned. "I heard you moving around and I wondered what was up. What do you mean? Is something wrong with your dad?"

"He's not here." Chloe swung her hands out in a helpless gesture. "Not in the study or the living room or the guest room. I'm afraid he and Lucinda may have had a fight last night and he took off."

"Don't panic—maybe he had an early morning business meeting," Nick suggested, but he looked worried too. "Come on, let's hit the kitchen. My brain doesn't work this early in the morning without caffeine." He pushed past her and started for the staircase. Suddenly, he stopped, his attention riveted to the door of the master bedroom. "Hang on," he said. He walked over to the bedroom door and slowly turned the handle.

Chloe wanted to ask what he thought he was doing, but she didn't want to make any noise. She watched silently as he eased the door open and stuck his eye to the crack. Then he pulled the door slowly shut and turned to face her. A huge grin was spread across his face.

"Well?" she hissed. "Don't keep me in suspense. What's up?"

"Your dad's in there," he said. "Right next to my mom. They're sleeping like babies."

"Thank goodness." Chloe sagged in relief. "I was scared he'd left."

"Come on." Nick laughed. "Let's get that coffee."

Nick was fairly handy around the kitchen, Chloe noticed. He had the coffee brewing in minutes.

"Do you think your mom and my dad have patched things up?" she asked. "I mean, after all, they were . . ." She jerked her head in the direction of the master bedroom.

"I hope so." He pulled a coffee mug out of the cupboard. "But it could just mean that they, uh, you know . . ."

She could feel herself blushing. "Yeah, I know. But I think it's a good sign, don't you?"

"It's a better sign than him not being here at all," Nick said cautiously. "But let's not get our hopes up. We don't know what happened here last night after we left."

"Well, it sure beats finding out that they had a knock-down-drag-out fight and he took off," she said. She walked over to the fridge and pulled out a carton of orange juice. "Want some?"

"Sure. It'll hold me till the coffee's ready. I always wake up thirsty." He slid onto a bar stool on the other side of the counter as she pulled a couple of glasses out of the dishwasher. "Don't you want to go upstairs and put on a robe or something?" he asked.

"Why?" Chloe shrugged and poured the juice. "I'm decent." The oversized nightshirt she wore was made of white, heavy cotton and reached to her knees.

"I know you are. But if your dad gets up, he'll freak if he finds you down here with me dressed like that." Nick yawned again. He had on a pair of cutoff jeans and a tank top.

"No he won't," she replied. "He's not that up-tight."

"Believe me, when it comes to his daughter, he is," he said. "I know how fathers think. No matter how innocent this is, he'll have a cow if you don't get some clothes on."

Chloe put the juice down and handed him his glass. This had to rank as one of the most bizarre conversations she'd ever had. Taking a sip from her glass, she shook her head. "He knows you don't like me."

"*Didn't* like you," Nick reminded her. "Past tense, remember? We've come a long way in the last few days. We're actually working together. Go on, it'll only take a minute. Get dressed. Besides, we need to discuss what's happened. I don't want to do that here." He glanced over his shoulder. "Your dad or my mom could barge in any second."

"You want to go outside?" she asked.

"Yeah, a long ways outside," he said. "I've got to drive over to my uncle's and work for a few hours this morning. Two of his men are sick and he's short-handed. You want to come with me? We could use some extra help."

Chloe's spirits soared. Then just as quickly she silently warned herself not to read anything into the invitation. Nick needed an extra pair of hands, that was all. She chugged back the last of her juice and set the glass down on the counter. "I've never worked on a ranch, but maybe it'll be fun. It'll be a new experience. Okay, I'll come with you. But I've got to be back in time to make dinner."

"Deal."

Chloe left the kitchen and hurried upstairs. She smiled to herself as she tiptoed past the master bedroom. She didn't see why Nick was such a doubting Thomas. Surely the two of them spending the night in the same room meant something.

She threw on a pair of jeans and a cotton blouse. As she ran a brush through her hair, she sighed softly. It would have been nice to have been invited because Nick wanted to be with her, but she wasn't going to kid herself on that score. His uncle needed help. Besides, she thought as she tossed the brush into her drawer, Nick was way out of her league.

She might have been the little rich girl, but he was the one who was genuinely sophisticated. He'd grown up in Los Angeles, knew how to pawn stuff, and had had his nose in a book since the first grade. Why would someone like him ever be attracted to someone like her? Chloe smiled sadly at her reflection. At least she was still pretty . . . there was no reason not to own up to that. It wasn't something she took any credit for anyway. Her looks were about the only thing she could offer someone like Nick. And he wasn't that shallow.

"Stop it," she told herself fiercely as she realized what she was thinking. There was nothing wrong with her. There was nothing wrong with anyone. If nothing else, she'd learned that from her trip down the tunnel.

She had plenty to offer another person. But she didn't think Nick would ever notice. Their relationship was simply too confusing.

She'd never, ever understand him. One minute he was as friendly as a Labrador pup and the next he was the iceman. Just last night, he'd barely spoken to her all the way home. And after she'd gone to all that trouble so he'd have a shot at getting to know Mia, too.

They discussed their parents on the drive to Bobby's ranch. "I still think it's too soon to be sure," Nick said. He pulled his car off the county highway and onto a long gravel driveway.

"But they spent the night together," she persisted. They'd been having this argument for the last ten miles. "And I think that means they're on the road to reconciliation."

"Please." Nick tossed her a pitying glance. "Take off the rose-colored glasses. All it means is that they spent the night in the same room. We don't even know that they did anything."

"Oh . . ." Chloe cringed. "Thinking about parents and sex is gross."

"You're the one who started it," he charged. "I'm the one who thinks we'd better come up with a strategy in case Tina and Jason really have flaked out and blown the rent money in Vegas." He pulled up in front of a large, white, ranch-style house, turned off the ignition, and climbed out.

The ranch was nestled at the top of a small hill. There was a large barn, a white-fenced corral, and a couple of smaller sheds nestled amongst a grove of California oak trees on the other side of the house.

"This place is gorgeous." Chloe got out her side and slammed the door.

"Yeah, Uncle Bobby works his tail off keeping it that way, too," Nick replied absently. "Anyway, what about Tina and Jason? What do you want to do?"

"What do you suggest? We can hardly sue."

"Don't I know it." Nick started for the barn. "But I've been thinking about our options."

She hurried to catch up with him. "We have options?"

"There are always options. As you pointed out, we can't exactly squeal on them, and they know it. I think we ought to make sure that if Mom takes it into her head to move, that I'm unavailable to help her."

"Unavailable how?" Chloe asked. "You live with her, remember?"

Nick laughed. "Yeah, but like I said, Uncle Bobby needs help. If Tina and Jason really have done a number on us, I'll tell Mom I've got to bunk over here for a while."

"Will she believe you?"

Nick stopped abruptly and turned to face her. "This is me we're talking about," he boasted, tapping himself on the chest. "I've never lied to my mom. She trusts me."

"And I'm sure my sister-in-law appreciates it," said an amused male voice.

Nick broke into a grin. "Hi, Uncle Bobby. This is Chloe. Do you remember her?"

"Sure do." Bobby Mallory nodded. "We met at the wedding. Nice to see you again, Chloe."

He kept his smile firmly in place, but Chloe could see the confusion in his eyes. As she'd barely been civil to the poor man at her father's wedding to Nick's mother, she realized she ought to be grateful he spoke to her at all. She was lucky he wasn't chasing her off his property with a pitchfork.

"It's nice to see you again, Mr. Mallory." She stepped over and extended her hand, wanting desperately to make up for her previous rude behavior. The fact that it had been well over a year ago didn't matter. "I hope you'll forgive me for the way I behaved the last time we met. I was terribly rude and I want you to know I'm really, really sorry."

"Gosh, little lady, you weren't that bad," he said, laughing as they shook hands. "Your nose was a bit out of joint and up in the air most of the time, but that's all. Welcome to my ranch. Did Nick bring you out to see the horses? He does that for some of his city friends. We're always glad to see them."

"I brought her out here to work," Nick said. "You told me on the phone yesterday that two of your hands are sick. I figured you could use all the help you could get."

"Do you know anything about horses?" Bobby asked Chloe.

She shook her head. "Not really, but I'm not afraid to learn."

"She can clean out the stables," Nick interjected. "Anyone can push a broom and shovel."

"Alrighty, then." Bobby laughed again. "Let's get started. Come on."

They headed toward the barn. Chloe took a deep breath as they went through the gate and into the barnyard. The air had a raw, earthy scent, a combination of grass and straw and manure. She kinda liked it. It smelled real. A lanky black dog, its tongue lolling out of its mouth, loped out of the barn toward them, heading straight for Nick. He seemed totally unconcerned about the eighty pounds of canine charging at him. Tail wagging furiously, the animal jumped up on its hind legs and licked Nick's face. "Down, Polly, down."

He introduced the dog to Chloe. "You're so cute," she exclaimed, patting the broad head.

"She's a ham," Bobby said. "She'll stay on your heels all day. This dog hasn't ever met a person she didn't like."

Bobby, with a bouncing Polly on his heels, led them past a huge round drinking trough and toward the barn proper. Chloe had never been to a place like this before. She found it fascinating. On one side there was a big loft that opened onto the yard. Inside, she could see bales of hay neatly stacked in huge, high rows. Next to the open loft was an oversized set of double doors that were at least twelve feet high. That's where Bobby took them.

As she stepped inside, Chloe blinked at the sudden dimness. There was a long, dusty cement corridor bisecting the room. Stalls lined each side of the corridor. She looked around, her gaze noting the clean, orderly open space directly to one side. It contained rows of shelves with saddles, bridles, brushes, buckets, and all sorts of things she couldn't even name.

Bobby and Nick had disappeared into the hayloft area.

"Hey, Nick," she called. "What's up?"

"I'm going to be grooming the horses," he announced as he came back into the barn. He had a shovel in one hand and a broom in the other. "Uncle Bobby has some buyers coming by later this afternoon. The horses and the barn need to be spruced up if he's going to make a good deal."

"Is that for me?" she asked curiously, pointing to the shovel.

"You got it." He started down the corridor to the first stall.

Chloe's eyes widened. There were piles of manure and dirty straw in the stall. Slowly, she held out her hand for the shovel. "Where do I put it?" she asked.

Nick laughed. "Man, I thought one look at this crap would have you running for the car." He thrust the broom and the shovel into her hands. "Good for you, Chloe, you proved me wrong."

"You're just glad I'm going to help," she said good-naturedly, but she allowed herself a small ray of hope at his words.

Maybe he didn't dislike her as much as she thought.

"Shovel it out into the corridor and then down to the end at the back of the barn," Nick instructed. "Uncle Bobby uses the manure as fertilizer."

"I can see why," she muttered.

"Thanks for giving us a hand," Nick said.

"No problem. I said I'd help and I will," she said,

wrinkling her nose. The smell was really quite strong. "But you're going to owe me big-time, Nick. Really big-time. This is good for at least one trip to the ice cream parlor. And you have to buy."

"You've got yourself a deal, kid."

CHAPTER EIGHT

Chloe's arms ached by the time Nick stuck his head in the barn and yelled that it was time to quit. She put the broom and the shovel neatly against the back door, brushed the dust off herself as best she could, and hurried out to the barnyard.

Just outside the door, she stopped. Nick was in the center of the barnyard. He was down on one knee, laughing and trying to wrest a ball out of Polly's mouth. The Lab shook her big head and dodged to the right. Then she spotted Chloe. She dropped the toy and dashed across the yard, her tail wagging furiously.

"Looks like you've made a real friend," Nick said as he grabbed at the bouncing ball. He caught it and rose to his feet. "Polly usually would rather play than eat."

Chloe braced herself as the dog jumped up and began licking her face. "Oh you cutie pie, you," she crooned as she petted Polly's head. "You're just the sweetest thing." She grinned at Nick. "She stayed in the barn with me. Every time I turned around, she'd be standing there with her tail wagging.''

Having a big dog so close would normally have frightened her—Chloe had never had a pet. But even though the first time she'd glanced over her shoulder and seen the dog standing there had startled her, she realized it was impossible to be scared of such a good-natured, tail-wagging, face-licking creature. She giggled and scratched the dog behind her ears. Polly closed her eyes and rolled her head to one side.

''When you two are finished with your mutual lovefest,'' Nick said, ''we'd better get going. If Uncle Bobby catches us here at lunchtime he'll make us eat the house special.''

Chloe laughed and gently pushed the animal down. ''What's that?''

''Believe me''—Nick pretended to shudder—''you don't want to know. Suffice to say he's been a bachelor a long time. His idea of getting rid of leftovers is to dump them all in one pot and cook it all day.''

''I heard that,'' Bobby called good-naturedly as he came out of the loft side of the barn. Polly abandoned her newfound friend and raced to her master. ''And I'll have you know, my cooking skills have improved enormously.''

''I'll bet they have. But we've got to get back, Uncle Bobby,'' Nick said quickly. He reached over, grabbed Chloe's hand, and tugged her in the direction of the car. ''Chloe's got KP duty at home and we've got some important stuff to do this afternoon.''

''What important stuff?'' Chloe asked.

''Calling Tina and Jason, for starters,'' he muttered.

"That's okay, kids," Bobby said. "Go on and get out of here. I appreciate all your help. Chloe"—he gave her a special grin—"you can come back anytime. Any friend of Polly's is a friend of mine."

"Thanks," she said with a laugh. "I'm glad your dog approves of me. It was fun, though. I enjoyed myself."

A few minutes later, they were in Nick's car and on the county road heading toward Landsdale. Chloe sighed happily. "That really was great."

"It was nice of you to help," Nick murmured. He shook his head. "I can't get over Polly. She usually won't budge from Uncle Bobby's side. Yet she clung to you like a burr."

"She left to go play ball with you," she reminded him.

"Only because I came to the door and bribed her with a dog biscuit," he admitted. He gave her a quick, assessing glance. "You used to be dead scared of animals. Remember the time last summer when you had hysterics over Mrs. Larkin's poodle?"

"That was one big poodle," Chloe said defensively, "and I didn't have hysterics, I merely left the vicinity quickly. If you'll recall, the dog tried to attack me. Besides, Mrs. Larkin shouldn't have brought him anyway. It was a cocktail reception, for goodness' sakes."

"Elmer just wanted one of your Swedish meatballs." Nick grinned. "And as I remember it, you took off like a bat out of hell before he got within ten feet of you." His smile disappeared and his expression turned thoughtful. "I didn't realize you were such an animal lover."

"I'm not. At least, I didn't use to be," Chloe admitted slowly. Come to think of it, there *was* something kind of weird the way the dog had hung around her. Every time she'd looked up or over her shoulder, the animal had been there, watching her with a silly, almost comical expression on its canine face.

"What do you mean?"

"I mean before the accident, before dying. You're right, you know—I *was* scared of animals. Especially dogs. But I'm not now. It's like I can sense how they feel—"

"You want to hit that ice cream parlor now?" he interrupted. "I don't know about you, but I could go for something cold."

She was a bit put out at his abruptness, but then she remembered he hated talking about her accident. Well, she thought, she couldn't really blame him— lots of people were squeamish. Especially when it came to talking about death.

"So could I," she agreed good-naturedly. "But . . ." She broke off and sniffed the air dramatically.

"Oh yeah." He laughed. "I guess maybe we ought to clean up a little. You do smell kinda ripe."

"You don't smell like a rose either." She poked him playfully on the arm.

They teased and bantered all the way home. By the time he pulled into the driveway, she was so relaxed with him it was like they'd known each other forever. She didn't want the feeling to stop. She liked it.

"I'll meet you at the car in fifteen minutes," he called over his shoulder as he took the stairs two at a time and disappeared down the hall to his room.

Chloe was showered, changed, and dressed in four-teen minutes flat. Nick was already in the car. She stopped in front of the decorator mirror in the foyer and tucked a stray strand of hair behind her ear. She wasn't sure if her good mood was caused by the fact that her plans were working out or by the fact that Nick was being so nice.

"It doesn't matter why I'm happy," she whispered to herself. "All that matters is it's working. I'm mak-ing up for all the mean things I did and soon Dad and Lucinda will come to their senses about this stupid divorce. Nick does like me, too. I know it."

But did she? She picked up her purse and turned to the front door. She didn't want to get her hopes up about him—that could lead to real heartbreak. Be-sides, just because they were working together didn't mean he'd really changed his opinion of her. After all, look at the way he hated talking about the acci-dent.

Her spirits sagged. Jeez, she was acting like a mo-ron. Of course he didn't believe her. He probably still thought her being nice was all an act. He was prob-ably just going along with it because he wanted his mother to be happy. It was impossible to tell what was going on with Nick or, for that matter, with any-one else. That was another downside to having been so selfish and self-centered—her ability to read other people was just about zero.

Chloe sighed again and stepped outside.

"Come on," he yelled from the car. "Let's get moving."

"Should we swing by and see if Mia wants to come?" she asked as she got inside and slammed the door. "She doesn't have much to do these days and her apartment is so hot."

Nick didn't say anything, but his mouth tightened.

Great, she thought, he doesn't believe I've changed, but when I try to show him what a decent person I can be, how I can put someone else's desires ahead of my own, he gets all uptight.

"If you don't want to," she began, "that's okay. I just thought you really liked Mia."

"What do you mean by that?" he asked sharply. He turned on the engine and pulled away from the curb.

Chloe realized she'd done it again. Totally misread the situation. Too bad they didn't give out an award for being insensitive—she'd win for sure. "I'm sorry, I've screwed up again, haven't I?" There was nothing else to do but be completely honest. "I thought you liked Mia—*really* liked her. You know, like you wanted to ask her out on a date or something."

"She's a nice person," he said, "but I don't have a crush on her or anything. Why on earth did you think I did?"

"Because of the way you used to give me such a hard time about her," Chloe explained. "You used to always claim I was using her. You were always saying how she was nice and smart and too good to hang out with someone like me." She took a deep breath, looked out her window so she wouldn't have to face him, and plunged on. "And even though I've had a crush on you for ages and ages, I thought that since my time here is temporary at best, and you're never going to like me anyway, I ought to do the right thing and fix you up with her. I think she really likes you. She's a great person. But every time I try to do it, you get all huffy and mad."

A low, strangled sound came from Nick's throat. Chloe turned her head sharply. "Hey," she yelped. "What are you doing? I thought we were going for ice cream."

Nick pulled the car over to the curb and killed the engine.

"Why'd you stop?" she asked. Crap, she hoped her honesty hadn't freaked him so badly he was going to throw her out of the car. Great, she said to herself as she looked out the window; just what she needed. Wouldn't you know it—he'd pulled over in front of Shawna's house. She'd love telling everyone at school that she saw Nick Mallory tossing Chloe Marlowe into the street. Then she told herself not to be so stupid. Nick wasn't mean; he wouldn't do something like that.

His mouth was open slightly and he was staring at her like she'd just announced she was an alien and shown him the tentacles hidden in her ear or something. "You're mad, aren't you?" she asked.

"Mad?" he asked with a shake of his head. "No. I'm confused and shocked and totally at a loss as to what to say to you."

"I'm sorry, I shouldn't have said anything. But I need to be honest," she explained.

"That's okay." He held up his hand. "I mean, I'm glad you're telling me how you feel. Did you mean it?"

"Mean what?"

"That you've had a crush on me?"

She could feel herself blushing. "Yeah," she mumbled.

"You sure didn't act like it." He turned on the ignition and pulled back out onto the road. "From the way you used to look down your nose at me, I thought you hated my guts."

"I was a wench," she said. "But you weren't exactly Mr. Nice Guy yourself." She'd suddenly realized that as selfish and creepy as she'd been, he hadn't gone out of his way to be all sweetness and light, either.

"Okay. We both could have been a little better to each other," he admitted. "But you started it. I was ready to be friends."

"You were kinda cold," she reminded him. That was true too. The first time she'd met Nick he'd barely spoken ten words to her.

"I wasn't cold, Chloe. I was nervous."

"Nervous? Why?"

He slowed the car as they reached the outskirts of the business section. "We're ordinary people. My mom might have worked in the entertainment industry, but we're still working people."

"I don't understand. My dad works. He works hard."

"I'm not saying he doesn't," Nick explained. "But he makes a helluva lot more money than most people.

You've seen our condo, Chloe. It's nice, but it's not a six-bedroom mansion like the one you live in. I was uptight because you and your old man were so rich. For crying out loud, you had a live-in housekeeper and a gardener.'' Turning on his blinker, he pulled into a small strip mall and parked in front of Edley's Ice Cream.

Chloe wasn't sure what to say, so she said nothing. Neither did Nick. They got out and went inside.

Nick stood in front of the high glass counter and studied the menu posted on the opposite wall like it was the lineups for the Super Bowl. Chloe figured he was embarrassed. That, or he didn't know what to make of her outburst or his own confession.

"What do you want?" he finally asked.

"Can I have a hot fudge sundae?" She might as well enjoy what pleasures she could in life, she decided.

Nick's eyebrows rose in surprise, but he turned to the kid behind the counter. "Two hot fudge sundaes."

"It'll be a minute," the boy said. "Go ahead and have a seat; I'll bring 'em over when they're ready."

Chloe started for a table close to the counter, but Nick grabbed her hand. "Not there. We've got some talking to do. We need privacy." He led her to a table as far away from the counter as possible.

"Now," he said as soon as they'd plopped down on the old-fashioned wrought-iron stools, "keep talking."

"Me?" she cried in surprise. "What about you?" Why should she be the only one to bare her soul?

"The only thing you've admitted to is being nervous."

He looked taken aback. "Yeah, okay, you're right." He shrugged. "I guess it is kinda my turn. Look, Chloe, I don't know what's going on here. I'm so confused I can't think straight, but there is one thing I want you to know. I don't hate you."

She cocked her head to one side and regarded him skeptically. "Are you sure?"

"I'm sure," he replied. "You've been a brat and you've done some really, really hateful things. But I'm coming around to believe you're really sorry."

"I *am* sorry," she insisted.

"Good, that's a start." He leaned back as their sundaes arrived. "And, uh, I'm sorry too."

"For what?"

He smiled briefly. "Like you said, I wasn't exactly Prince Charming when we first met." He leaned back, taking his elbows off the table as the sundaes were placed in front of them.

"Wow. These look great." Chloe smiled brightly at the waiter. She vaguely recognized him. "Do you go to Landsdale High?"

The boy blushed all the way to the roots of his light brown hair. "I'm a sophomore," he said shyly.

"My name's Chloe Marlowe," she continued. "Nice to meet you."

"I'm Tad McAdams," he replied. "Uh, will there be anything else?"

"This is fine," Nick said quickly. He shot Chloe an irritated glance. She blithely ignored it.

"Thank you," she said to Tad as he went back

behind the counter. "There was no need to be rude," she hissed at Nick. "He's just trying to do his job and make a living. Not everyone was born with a silver spoon in their mouth, you know."

Nick's jaw dropped. "Coming from you, that's rich. Since when have you become such a champion of the working class? . . . Oh, never mind, I know, since you died."

"As a matter of fact, yes." She picked up her spoon and took a huge bite of her sundae. "Mmmm . . . this is good."

Nick shook his head. "God, I still don't understand it, but you must have changed. That's all I can say."

"Well, it's about time you started believing me," she stated. "When did the miracle occur? Was it because you've noticed how kind I'm trying to be to everyone? How helpful?"

"You can fake being kind and helpful," he retorted cheerfully. "But you can't fake *that*." He jerked his chin toward her sundae.

"Huh?"

Nick grinned. "The old Chloe was practically anorexic. You were so paranoid about not being about to get your butt into a size eight, you picked at your food like a bird. Now, every time I see you you're stuffing your face. I figure it had to be something cosmic to make that happen."

She laughed and made a face at him. Maybe things would work out fine. Maybe he was coming to really like her. Then she sobered as she remembered the one subject they'd both tried to avoid today. "What are we going to do about Tina and Jason?"

"There's nothing we can do," Nick replied. "I called the condo last night. All I got was their answering machine."

"Did you leave a message?"

"No, I didn't want them calling the house and Mom picking up the phone. What could we say if she asked why Tina or Jason was calling to speak to me?"

Chloe nodded. She too had given the problem a lot of thought. That was one of the reasons she'd gotten up so early today. "You know, we might be making a mountain out of a molehill," she said. That was one of Carlotta's favorite expressions.

"You think everything's okay because our parents spent the night in the same room—" he began.

"I think it's a good start," Chloe interrupted him. "In case you haven't noticed, our parents are being really civilized about this divorce."

"So?" he challenged.

"So your mom isn't the kind of person to do something impulsively. . . . If she and my dad spent the night together it's because they talked out their differences. I know I'm right, Nick. I can feel it."

Nick smiled sadly. "Did dying make you psychic?"

"Sort of," she replied.

"I was being sarcastic," he said.

"I know." She grinned. "Anyway, I know I'm right."

Nick smiled back at her. "You might be right, but just in case there's a problem, I'm going to keep trying to reach Tina and Jason."

"That's fair," Chloe said. She concentrated on en-

joying her ice cream. She smiled softly and scraped
the bottom of the dish, scooping out the last of the
hot fudge.

"You about ready to go?" Nick asked. "I'll drop
you off at the house. I've got to get back to Uncle
Bobby's. He wants me to help him move some live-
stock later this afternoon."

"Is there anything I can do?" she asked. "I liked
working out there."

"Nah, you did enough this morning. But it's nice
of you to offer," Nick said as they stepped outside
into the bright sunshine and headed for his car.
"We'll be on horseback for this job. It'll be kinda
tough, even for someone like me who's used to riding."

They didn't talk much on the drive home. Chloe
didn't mind. She wanted a few minutes to think. Mentally, she began ticking off her good deeds. The things
she'd done to atone for her crummy past.

First of all, she was fairly sure she'd talked her dad
out of suing the county. At least he hadn't mentioned
it again. Then, of course, there was Carlotta. Carlotta
would undoubtedly take a while to warm up to her,
but Chloe felt good that the housekeeper was spending her free time at her sister's. Besides, she told herself, even when Carlotta was back and running the
house, Chloe still intended to do her fair share of helping with the cooking and cleaning. Carlotta wasn't
any spring chicken.

Mia seemed to believe her—that meant a lot to
Chloe. She was so glad she'd been honest with her.
She was downright lucky to have a friend like Mia.

She glanced over at Nick as he turned the car into their street. She was suddenly deeply embarrassed that she'd admitted to him she'd had a crush on him these many months. She wasn't worried about it making him conceited—Nick wasn't the kind to let a few words of praise go to his head. But she was concerned he'd be uptight about hurting her and that then he'd start to avoid her.

Chloe didn't want that to happen. "There's something I need to tell you," she blurted as he pulled the car into the driveway.

Nick shut off the engine and turned to her. "Yeah? Look, Chloe, I'm not sure how many more revelations of yours I can take."

"This is no big deal," she promised. Not to him, anyway; it was to her. "But I want you to know that whatever happens between us, I really value our relationship and I hope we'll always be friends."

He didn't say anything for a minute, just stared at her. Finally he sighed. "Sure, we'll be friends."

"Okay," she muttered. She had a feeling she'd blown it again, and she wasn't sure why. He wasn't breathing fire, but he didn't look happy. She fumbled for the handle on the car, finally found the darned thing and wrenched the door open. She'd started to get out when she felt his hand on her arm.

"Wait a minute," he said.

She turned and braced herself for another lecture.

"Would you go to the movies with me on Wednesday night? Carlotta should be back by then, so we won't have to hang around the house while you cook dinner."

Chloe's jaw dropped.

• • •

Chloe spent the rest of the afternoon vacuuming, dusting, and cleaning the kitchen. She wasn't very good at it, but she didn't let that stop her. She just doggedly kept at it until things at least *looked* clean.

She'd swiped the kitchen counter for the tenth time when the phone rang.

"Hi, Chloe, it's Mia. What are you doing today?"

"Cleaning," she replied. She had a fast, ugly flash of guilt as she remembered Nick asking her for a date. Maybe Nick wasn't romantically interested in Mia, but Mia sure liked him. "Uh, I need to ask you something and I need you to be really honest with me."

"What?" Mia asked innocently.

"Would you mind if I went out with Nick?" Chloe was determined to be honest. "I mean, would it bother you?"

It took Mia a moment to answer. "Why should it?" she asked. "I think he's cute and all that. I'll even admit to having a crush on him, but I'm not in love with him or anything. Why do you ask? Has he asked you for a date?"

"We're going to the movies on Wednesday," she replied. "I didn't want you feeling bad about it."

"Don't sweat it," Mia said flippantly. But beneath her tone, Chloe sensed, her friend was miserable.

"Nick's a hunk and all that," Mia continued, "but there's dozens of them out there. What are you going to do if that guy you met at the bookstore calls?"

"Who? Oh, you mean Jed." It took a moment before Chloe understood. When she finally realized just who Mia was referring to, she had a wonderful idea.

"He's not interested in me. He was just being nice and helping me with some info, that's all. Uh, look, he's a really cute guy. Would you like to meet him? We could all get together for coffee or something."

Mia snorted faintly. "Hey, maybe I'm not as gorgeous as you, but I don't need your castoffs."

Shocked, Chloe gasped. She couldn't believe what her friend had just said. "I didn't mean it like that," she protested, "and you're every bit as pretty as me. Prettier, probably. I just thought you'd like to meet Jed. He's nice and good looking—"

"I know what you thought," Mia interrupted. "But I don't need your pity castoffs. I can get my own dates."

"This isn't a pity castoff," she cried. "I was just trying to bring together two people who I thought might like each other." Chloe felt like a worm. Why hadn't she kept her mouth shut? Her day was going so good, too. She was sure things were finally working out. "Besides, I'm not sure he's going to call at all." Chloe turned as she heard a car honking. The sound was coming from her driveway. She stood on tiptoe and peered out the window. Carlotta's big Buick was there. Damn. She really needed to sort this out with Mia.

Carlotta honked again.

"Shoot," Chloe said. "I've got to go—Carlotta's back early and she's outside honking. I think something's wrong. But we've got to talk. I don't want you mad at me."

"I'm not mad," Mia muttered. "Call me later."

"Okay. Honestly, I just thought you might like this

guy.'' She put down the phone and dashed outside just as Carlotta hit the horn again.

"Hi, Chloe," Carlotta said glumly. She opened the car door.

"What are you doing back so early?" she asked. "You're not due back till tomorrow night."

"Come over here and give me a hand," Carlotta ordered.

Chloe, with a sinking feeling in her stomach, flew over to the car and peeked over the open driver's door. The housekeeper's left ankle was tightly bound in an Ace bandage. "Oh no. What happened?"

"Take a wild guess," Carlotta grumbled. "I sprained my ankle going down Elvira's patio stairs— it was pouring cats and dogs down there. I wasn't doing my sister any good, so I decided to come home." She leaned halfway out of the car and held out her arm. "Give me a hand, will you. It hurts to walk on this thing."

Chloe eased in and draped the housekeeper's arm over her shoulder. "Don't forget my cane," Carlotta said.

"I'll come back out and get it when I bring in your suitcase," Chloe assured her. Moving slowly, they managed to get Carlotta into the house and onto a kitchen stool.

"Oh, that feels better," Carlotta mumbled. "Thank God it was my left ankle and I could still drive."

"Good thing your car isn't a stick shift," Chloe said brightly.

"Yeah, thank God for small favors," Carlotta muttered darkly.

"I'm so sorry," Chloe said. "This must be absolutely miserable for you." Things were going to Hades in a handbasket pretty fast. Her best friend was mad at her and now poor Carlotta was home with a sprained ankle. Why did she suddenly feel like both of these events were her fault? "Do you want me to get you some ice? Uh, should I make some coffee?"

Carlotta winced. "I've had enough coffee to float a battleship. I'll just rest here a minute and then you can help me to my room."

"I'll get your stuff from the car." Chloe leapt to her feet and dashed for the kitchen door. "Oh, Carlotta, this is all my fault. I'm so sorry. If I hadn't insisted you go visit your sister, you wouldn't have sprained your ankle."

Carlotta shook her head and smiled wanly, but Chloe didn't see it. She was already outside.

She started toward the car just as her father pulled into the driveway. Chloe waved, but he didn't wave back. He was too busy talking to Lucinda. He jammed on the brakes suddenly and she realized that he hadn't seen Carlotta's car. Then he jerked open the door and got out. "Hi, Dad," Chloe called. "Uh, Carlotta's back. I'll move her car as soon as I get her suitcase out."

Her father ignored her. "That's the most ridiculous thing I've ever heard," he yelled. Lucinda got out her side of the car and slammed the door.

" 'Ridiculous,' " Lucinda snapped. "It's nowhere near as ridiculous as what you've proposed. Why shouldn't I take that job?"

"You don't have to work," he snapped back. He

stalked up the driveway toward the back door. "There's no reason for you to drive all the way down there every day just to spite me."

"There's every reason," Lucinda stormed, right on his heels. "It's not like I can trust you."

"Uh, hi," Chloe said. "I guess you two have a lot to talk about. Well, I'll just grab the suitcase and Carlotta's cane and get out of your way."

Lucinda flashed her an angry glare as she stormed into the house. So did her father. Chloe's shoulders sagged. It didn't look like her father and Lucinda were on the road to reconciliation.

Well, crap, she thought, so far she was batting three out of three. First Mia got in a snit, then Carlotta came home with a sprained ankle, and now this.

Her good intentions were in the toilet, that was for sure. What on earth was she going to do now?

CHAPTER
NINE

Chloe got Carlotta's suitcase out of the backseat, snatched the cane out of the front, slammed the door, and trudged back into the kitchen.

She smiled at the housekeeper. "Here's your stuff. I'll take it to your room for you, okay?"

Stony faced, Carlotta stared back at her. "I shoulda stayed here instead of going to my sister's. Those damned stairs of hers are slippery as all get-out." She pursed her lips and jerked her head toward the front of the house. Dan's and Lucinda's angry voices could still be heard as they carried their argument into the den. "Your dad's sure in a bad mood. I hope he doesn't can me because of this stupid ankle."

Chloe's heart sank even lower. This was great, just great. Mia was ticked, Carlotta was sweating being unemployed, and her dad and Lucinda were at each other's throats. She couldn't even reassure the housekeeper that her father wouldn't dare fire her. Chloe was fairly certain her father wouldn't do something that stupid, but then again, she hadn't thought he'd be dumb enough to want to divorce Lucinda either. "Uh, would you like me to take your suitcase now? I'm sure you don't want to listen to my dad screaming his head off."

Carlotta shrugged. Chloe grabbed the case and scurried off. She put the bag next to Carlotta's neatly made twin and took her sweet time getting back to the kitchen. Her stomach was in knots.

As she walked down the hall, she could hear her dad's angry accusations and Lucinda's furious replies. Somehow, she knew this was her fault too.

She had to think. She had to figure out a way to fix things. But who could think with World War Three being fought just down the hall? "This is ridiculous," she muttered. "I've got to get out of here." Glancing at her watch, she realized she had time to go for a walk while supper was in the oven. The way things were going, it didn't look like anyone would be much in the mood for a family dinner anyway. If she was a bit late getting something on the table, it wouldn't matter.

"Would you like a cup of tea or something?" she asked Carlotta as she came back into the kitchen.

"That'd be nice."

"Good." Chloe put the water on to boil, pulled a mug out of the cupboard, and dropped a tea bag inside. "As soon as the tea's ready, I'll help you to your room. You probably want to rest."

"You don't have to do that," Carlotta said. "I can get around on my own. It's just getting in and out of the car that's hard. I've got to get dinner ready."

"No you don't," Chloe said. She figured she might

as well stick to her guns, even though it didn't seem there was anything she could say or do for the house-keeper that was likely to make the woman think any better of her. "You've got to rest that ankle so it gets better. Dinner is a cinch. There's a chicken marinating in the fridge, baking potatoes scrubbed, and a salad all made up. I'll put the food in the oven before I go out and put it on the table when I get back."

"So you're going out?"

"Just for a walk," Chloe said. "I've got a lot of thinking to do."

Chloe sighed as she left the house. Her father and Lucinda were still arguing, Carlotta was complaining bitterly about her sore foot, and to top it off, Nick had called and said he wouldn't be home for dinner. Well, great, she thought as she took off down the street at a brisk pace. Just great. Nothing, and I mean nothing, has gone right.

She hurried down the main road leading out of the housing tract. She couldn't believe how things had gotten so messed up so quickly. Chloe came to the entrance to the tract and turned out onto Camden Road. To her left, the road was dead straight for a good half mile, curving only to go round the base of the nearby foothills. Except for a couple of old apart-ment houses, they lived in virtually the last housing tract out of town. Beyond it, there was nothing but the wilderness of the semiarid desert that was South-ern California. Dead ahead, there was a crosswalk leading to a nature trail that ran alongside the creek bed. Chloe hurried to the crosswalk, jabbed the button for a green light, and then stalked across.

Chloe started to turn the other way, to go toward town instead of away from it, when something caused her to change her mind. For no apparent reason, she whirled and headed in the other direction.

She narrowed her eyes against the glare of the sun reflecting off the chrome of the cars and trucks whizzing past. Camden Road connected with the freeway less than a mile up the road, just past the spot where she'd driven her car into a tree. The road was old and narrow, one lane in each direction, but that didn't stop people from going too fast.

Houses from her tract climbed up the hill in neat, tidy rows. Beyond that were a few older apartment houses that had been here since the sixties. Mainly, they housed lower-income families and migrant workers who worked the fields over near Oxnard. Ahead of her, the foothills meandered toward the mountains. The hot sun beat down on her, but she kept walking. Her mind worked furiously with each step she took. What was she going to do? Everything had fallen apart . . . and so darn quickly, too.

Idly, she noted a little boy coming down the stairs of the apartment house nearest the road. She was too far away to see him all that clearly, but he didn't look old enough to be out on his own.

Perspiration dripped down her back as she trudged onward. No matter how many times she thought about her problems, she simply couldn't see any solutions. All of her intentions had been so good. She'd only wanted to help people. To atone. Instead, she'd messed up. Jeez, she might as well have stayed the old Chloe. No, that isn't true, she thought. Maybe some of the stuff she'd tried to do hadn't worked out like she'd planned, but her motives had been good.

She stopped, turned, and thought about heading back. There was no point getting sunstroke over this. Maybe by now her dad and Lucinda would have finished their argument. She started to go back the way she'd come when something made her turn and look.

The little boy was now off the steps and heading for the busy road. Chloe bit her lip and scanned the area. Surely his mom was somewhere around? But the small, asphalt parking lot in front of the apartment house was empty and there was no one on the stairs.

Someone'll come, she told herself as she started walking toward the kid. But none of the apartment doors opened and no anxious mother stuck her head out.

The little boy had stopped at the edge of the road, bent down, and was picking at something in the grass. Now that she was closer, she could see that he was no more than two.

She started to walk faster.

From down the narrow road, she could see a huge truck speeding toward them.

The little boy straightened up.

"Hey," she yelled, "get back."

The kid totally ignored her.

Chloe started to run.

The truck was getting closer and closer.

The boy stepped off the grassy verge.

Chloe's heart rammed into her throat. She hesitated for a split second. But only for a second; then she put on speed, giving it everything she had. She wasn't going to make it. The dumb kid was going to step in front of an eighteen wheeler right before her eyes. "Get back!" she screamed.

The kid finally turned and looked at her. She was close enough now to see his eyes widen in fright. He screamed and backed up . . . not toward the grassy verge, but farther into the road.

The trucker finally saw the kid. He blasted his horn and laid on his brakes. The kid, really scared now, stumbled even farther into the road.

"Oh God," Chloe prayed as she ran, "please let me make it."

Her side ached, her ankle turned, and she staggered, but she kept on going. The truck was slowing, but not enough. Honking furiously, the big metal monster came careening toward the terrified child.

Chloe was close, so close. But not close enough.

Everything began to happen in slow motion. From far away, she heard a woman screaming. Chloe was acting on impulse, not thinking, letting her instincts guide her. She dived for the child, grabbed him in her arms, and rolled to the other side of the road just as the truck whizzed past.

The world righted itself.

Two people, a man and woman, charged at her.

"Oh my God. Oh my God," the woman screamed hysterically.

"Is he all right? Is he all right?" The man reached them first. He yanked the child out of Chloe's arms and held him close. The woman fell on them a second later. All three of them were crying.

Chloe lay where she was a moment, trying to catch her breath and taking inventory of her body parts.

"That was one brave thing you did, kid." A hand came out of nowhere and helped her to her feet. Chloe looked up into the frightened face of the truck driver. He'd managed to pull his rig over to the side of the road. "You okay?"

Gratefully, she nodded. "I think so." She groaned. Both her knees were badly scraped. Her hip hurt, her right arm had lost a patch of skin on the elbow, and her lungs felt like they'd been seared with tar. But the boy was okay. That was what was important.

Suddenly all her aches and pains seemed to recede as a sense of peace descended on her. The trucker walked over to the group huddled on the side of the road. Chloe vaguely heard them talking, but she didn't pay much attention. The child had been saved. She, Chloe Marlowe, had saved another human being's life.

She knew exactly what that meant. She'd done what she'd been sent back to do.

"I really admire you, kid." The trucker pulled the big rig up the hill into the housing tract. "You've got more guts than I have. I don't think I'd have had enough nerve to jump in front of a monster like this." He tapped his steering wheel. "Which street is it?"

"The last one at the top of the hill," she said. "But you can pull over and drop me off right up there." She pointed to a spot in the road. "Then you can cut down Lyman Way and that'll take you back out. You won't have to try and turn this thing around."

The man had insisted on giving her a lift home. Chloe had been glad of his kindness. Her knees were still a bit shaky. But all's well that ends well, she told herself.

The parents, Bill and Lorie Nelson, had been hysterically grateful. Tommy, their little boy, had wandered outside not because his folks were irresponsible flakes, but because each parent thought he was with the other. When Mrs. Nelson came out of the bedroom and realized Tommy wasn't sitting on her husband's lap watching TV, they'd started searching. They'd seen Chloe save their son's life.

The trucker pulled the rig over and Chloe, with more thanks and a wave of her hand, got out. Her whole body ached as she walked home.

The house was quiet when she let herself in the front door. She went to the kitchen. There was a note from Carlotta stuck on the fridge for her. "Chloe, just put the food on the counter. Your father says we can help ourselves when we get hungry."

"So much for happy families eating meals together," she muttered. She checked the potatoes and chicken, closed the oven, and then went upstairs to shower and take care of her wounds.

By the time she came back downstairs, her knees had stopped stinging from the antiseptic and she could walk without limping. She quickly put the food out and got down plates, silverware, and napkins. People could just help themselves, she decided.

"Aren't you hot?" Carlotta asked as she hobbled into the kitchen on her cane.

Chloe looked down at the long robe she'd thrown

on after her shower, which she'd worn deliberately to hide her cuts and bruises. She'd decided not to mention what had happened this afternoon. Considering what a grim mood her dad was in, he might want to sue or prosecute or do something else equally stupid if he knew how close she'd come to meeting the grim reaper for a second time. "No. I'm wearing this because it's cozy. Would you like me to fix you a plate?"

"No." The housekeeper smiled warmly. "You've done more than your fair share." She propped her cane against the wall and swung herself up on one of the stools on the other side of the counter.

"Should I leave this stuff out?" Chloe glanced toward the front of the house. "I mean, is anyone going to eat?"

Carlotta laughed. "They'll eat later if they get hungry. Both of them are too busy licking their wounds to worry about their stomachs."

"That bad, huh?"

"Worst fight I've ever heard them have," Carlotta replied softly. "But maybe it cleared the air some. I don't know—they've always been way too polite to each other. Maybe it did them some good to have a good old screaming match."

Chloe didn't think so, but she wasn't going to discuss it. "Is Dad in the den?"

"He's upstairs. So's Lucinda." Carlotta laughed again. "Take that worried look off your face, girl. They ain't killed each other. I think they're talking."

Chloe started for the hall. "Maybe I'll let them know that the food's ready."

"Come on back here," Carlotta ordered. "They'll eat when they're good and ready. I want to talk to you."

"You want to talk to me?" Chloe wasn't sure she liked the sound of that. But she crossed over and sat down on a stool next to the housekeeper.

Carlotta reached over and patted her hand. "I just want to tell you I really appreciate what you've done. It's meant a lot to me, knowing that I can go to Elvira's every weekend if I want—"

"Oh, but you sprained your ankle," Chloe interrupted. "And I feel so bad about that. . . ."

"Why?" Carlotta demanded. "It wasn't your fault. It was mine for not paying attention to where I was going."

"It *was* my fault," Chloe countered. "If I hadn't insisted you go, you wouldn't have slipped on those wet patio stairs."

"Don't be silly, girl." She shook her head vigorously. "I went of my own free will. You didn't put a gun to my head and make me go. It was my own fault for not paying attention to where I was going. . . ."

"Really? You don't blame me?"

"Blame you?" Carlotta frowned in confusion. "Is that what you thought? That I blamed you?"

"Well, I've done so many awful things," Chloe said. "And I really wanted to make up for it. But when you hurt yourself, I thought it would only be natural that you'd think it was my fault. And I felt so bad; I had such good intentions—"

"The road to hell is paved with good intentions,"

Carlotta said. "Sorry, didn't mean to interrupt you. I just couldn't help it."

Chloe thought for a moment. "Do you really think that's true?"

"Of course not. I don't think someone with good intentions is on the road to hell." Carlotta eased off the stool and reached for her cane. "But I do believe in the Law of Unintended Consequences." She hobbled toward the center island.

"What's that?" Chloe got up and trailed after her.

Carlotta laughed. "Exactly what it says. You do something and you think it'll make things turn out a certain way. Most of the time, you're right—things do turn out like you'd expect. But there's always unintended results to your actions. They aren't necessarily good and they aren't necessarily bad, they're just there."

"I'm not sure I follow you."

"Here, let me give you an example. Your good intention was to give me weekends off to visit my sister, right? The unintended consequence of that visit is that I sprained my ankle."

"And you're worried you'll lose your job," Chloe said quickly. "But don't worry, please. I'll make sure my dad doesn't do anything rash. We couldn't get along without you around here."

"Quit putting words in my mouth. I'm not worried about gettin' fired. I wasn't really worried earlier, I was just venting steam." She propped her cane against the wall of the island and reached for a plate. "My point was, the unintended consequence of my visit to my sister wasn't that I'd lose my job, but that

I'd sprain my ankle. No one is to blame for that. It was just an accident. But it happened. That's what I mean about the Law of Unintended Consequences. As for you, young lady''—she grinned and popped a baked potato onto her plate—''you've changed. Really changed. And I don't think you'll ever go back to being like you was before. You know''—Carlotta put her plate down and looked away, gazing out the window over the sink—''I worked for your family before your mom died.''

Chloe felt a lump rise in her throat. Carlotta had never spoken to her about her mother. ''I remember. We lived in that house over on Dayton Street.''

''It was a nice little house,'' the housekeeper mused. ''Not big and fancy like this one. I started working for your folks when your mom got so sick.'' She turned and looked at Chloe. ''Your mother was a wonderful woman. One of the nicest people I'd ever met. I want you to know you've turned into a young woman she'd have been real proud of.''

Chloe blinked hard to hold back the tears. For some reason, knowing her mother would have approved of her made everything all right. ''Thank you for telling me.''

''Now take that worried expression off your face and grab a plate. This chicken smells too good to waste.''

Chloe and Carlotta ate in companionable silence. Chloe cleared up and loaded things in the dishwasher. She nodded at the platters of food left on the island counter. ''Should I leave this stuff out?''

''No, I don't think your dad and stepmom are going

to be down for quite a while, and Nick won't be home till real late. Let's just cover this stuff good and pop it in the fridge. If anyone's hungry, they can fix themselves a plate and microwave it.''

"You spoke to Nick?'' Chloe asked eagerly. "Is he okay?''

"He called while you were out on your walk. He's fine. He's helping his uncle set up a computerized bookkeeping system for the ranch. He said he might not be home at all tonight, that he might bunk there. Now.'' Carlotta made a shooing motion with her hands. "You go on upstairs and do whatever it is you do in that room of yours. You look tired.''

"I'll help put the food away,'' Chloe offered.

"No, no, you've done enough.'' Carlotta pointed to the door. "Don't worry about my darned ankle. I'm fine. You go.''

"Oh, all right. But call me if you need me,'' Chloe said as she headed for the hallway. She was disappointed. Not because she wasn't going to be doing kitchen duty, but because she'd wanted to see Nick.

But perhaps it was just as well that he wasn't around. Carlotta had given her lots to think about. Unintended consequences. Chloe paused at the bottom of the stairs. That was an interesting thought. Scary even. If every action had consequences you couldn't predict, that would mean that no one should do anything. But that wouldn't work, either, she told herself. She'd started up the stairs when the doorbell rang. "I'll get it,'' she called quickly.

Chloe pulled the door open. "Hi.'' Mia stood there, smiling at her shyly. "Can I come in?''

"Sure."

"Are you going to bed?" Mia asked. She looked pointedly at Chloe's robe. "I was hoping we could hang out and talk for a while."

"I'm not going to bed. I just threw this on when I got out of the shower. Let's go upstairs."

Chloe winced as her aching muscles protested climbing the stairs. But she was careful to keep her expression bland. She didn't want to let her pain show. She'd decided not to tell Mia about this afternoon. Her instincts warned her that she shouldn't tell anyone what had happened.

It was simply too private. Too personal. Chloe didn't understand what made her feel that way, but she'd learned to trust her instincts.

"Make yourself comfortable," Chloe said. She flopped on the bed.

Mia sat down on the end but didn't look at her. She sighed and smoothed nonexistent wrinkles. Finally, she looked at Chloe and said, "I came to apologize."

"For what?" Chloe wondered if there was something in the air. First Carlotta and now Mia.

"For being such a cow." Mia smiled sadly. "You were trying to do me a favor and I was such a bitch."

"Hey, you weren't being a bitch. I shouldn't have tried to set you up with someone neither of us even knows. That was dumb, real dumb."

"But your intentions were good," Mia protested.

"And the road to hell is paved with good intentions," Chloe shot back, repeating Carlotta's words. "Anyway, I'm really sorry. I'll never do it again."

"Never is a long time." Mia grinned. "Besides,

you're not the only one who's sorry. The truth is, I was jealous of you and Nick. I was hoping he'd like me.''

"He does like you," Chloe assured her.

"Yeah, but just as a friend. I mean, he's not interested in dating or anything. I shouldn't have gotten my hopes up. It was really stupid. But he was so nice when we went out for ice cream the other evening. I guess I kinda imagined he liked me more than he does.''

"I'm sorry." Chloe sighed. "I guess that's my fault. I was kinda trying to bring you two together.''

"Why?" Mia asked. "I mean, had he ever indicated he wanted to date me?''

"No, but he was always telling me that I didn't deserve to have a friend like you," she answered honestly. "And I thought that meant he had a crush on you.''

"But he didn't, did he?''

"No. Nick thought I didn't deserve having your friendship because I wasn't much of a friend to you." Chloe clamped her mouth shut. She didn't want to go too far. Mia's feelings were fragile and Chloe didn't want to hurt them needlessly. Drat, maybe that was another unintended consequence. Maybe Mia had secretly hoped that Nick liked her and now her hopes were crushed. Now that Chloe understood about unintended consequences, she wasn't so sure that brutal honesty was always the best policy.

The two girls stared at each other for a few moments. Then Mia's mouth curved into a wide grin and she burst out laughing. "Oh jeez, you weren't that bad, Chloe. Honestly. You were a bit self-centered at times, but you weren't the Wicked Witch of the West.''

Chloe relaxed. ''Good. I'm glad you think I wasn't so awful, and I have tried to make up for it.''

''Your efforts have been duly noted,'' Mia said. ''Anyway, one of the other reasons I came over tonight is to tell you about Steve Rimmer.''

''Who's that?''

''The guy who lives downstairs from me,'' Mia said. ''I've mentioned him before. He's the real good-looking one who goes to Landsdale JC.''

''You mean the hunk?''

Mia giggled. ''Yeah. Anyhow, to make a long story short, he asked me out for tomorrow night.''

''That's great!'' Chloe enthused. ''Where's he taking you? Dinner and a movie?''

''Better than that. Dinner and a play.'' She giggled excitedly. ''That's how come he asked me out. He saw me reading *Our Town* down in the laundry room last week. The college just happens to be putting it on and he asked me if I wanted to go. He's really neat, Chloe. He's real shy, though. He told me it took him almost a week to work up the nerve to ask me to go.''

''That is so fabulous,'' Chloe exclaimed. She leapt to her feet. ''Hang on, don't say another word. I'm going to get us a couple of sodas and then you can tell me all the details. I want to hear everything.''

Chloe woke up the next morning at the crack of dawn. She lay in her bed for a moment, trying to pinpoint why she felt so uneasy. She knew she should be feeling pretty good. Mia wasn't mad at her anymore and even Carlotta had come around. Or at least now she didn't think Chloe was totally spoiled and hopeless.

But there was still the big one out there. Her father and Lucinda. What was happening? She hadn't heard a peep out of either of them all evening.

Mia had stayed until almost eleven and in that time, neither her dad nor Lucinda had left the master bedroom, even to grab a bite of dinner. Chloe had a bad feeling about this. When people talked that long and that seriously without screaming their heads off, it usually meant trouble. She hoped they hadn't talked themselves past the point of no return.

Darn. She really needed to talk to Nick. Maybe he'd had some word from Tina and Jason? Maybe he had some idea what to do? She sighed and pushed the covers aside. Walking to the window, she peeked out through the blinds. The sun was barely cresting the eastern mountains. Blast. She couldn't go busting into Nick's room now. It was way too early. It had been well past midnight when she'd heard him come in last night. He'd worked all day at his uncle's, and he was probably dead tired. Chloe knew what that felt like. Her own workout cleaning that barn, coupled with her fast dive in front of a speeding truck had taken its toll on her stamina. Once she'd known Nick was safely home, she'd slept like a log.

She tried to think what to do. If Tina and Jason didn't turn up with the rent, Lucinda would be moving out of here in a few days. Once that happened, the odds of them patching up their marriage went way down.

Wide awake, Chloe stared at the far wall. She didn't want to hang around twiddling her thumbs. She had too much energy for that. Yet it might be hours before anyone else was up. She glanced out the window again and made up her mind. It was cool, quiet, and peaceful out there. Just what she needed. There was something serious she had to think about, something she'd been hiding from since yesterday afternoon. She'd go for another walk. Not only would that work off her excess energy, but it would give her a chance to think without any distractions.

And she knew just where she'd walk to. The place where it all began.

"Have you seen Chloe?" Nick asked. Yawning, he stumbled into the kitchen and plopped down on a stool.

"She's probably still asleep," Carlotta replied. "You want some coffee?"

"That'd be great." He yawned again. "She's not in her room—I checked. She was here last night, wasn't she?"

"Yes. She cooked a nice supper—not that anyone but me and her ate it—and then her friend came over. Why do you ask?" Carlotta handed him a mug of coffee.

"I just wondered, that's all. Her bed's all made, so I thought maybe she'd gone to one of her friends for the night."

"Her bed's made?" Carlotta frowned and reached for her cane. She hobbled toward the back window.

"What's wrong with your foot?" Nick asked.

"I sprained it at my sister's yesterday." She pushed the curtains aside and peered out. "She's not on the patio or in the pool."

"Then where is she?" Nick knew he shouldn't be worried, but all of a sudden, he was.

"That's what I'd like to know," Carlotta muttered as she hobbled back. "She's been acting funny ever since she had that accident."

"Who's been acting funny?" Dan asked cheerfully as he came into the kitchen. "Good morning, everyone, isn't it a lovely day?"

Nick and Carlotta both stared at him. Dan chuckled, patted his stepson on the back, and headed for the coffee. "You sit down, Carlotta," he ordered the housekeeper as she attempted to beat him to the pot. "With that ankle of yours, you don't have to wait on me. As a matter of fact, I don't want you bothering with doing any housework or cooking, either.''

''I don't want Chloe getting stuck with all the work,'' Carlotta retorted. ''My ankle isn't that bad; I can manage.''

''You don't have to,'' Dan said as he poured his coffee. ''The house is clean enough and everyone can handle their own laundry. As for the cooking, you've got the night off. Lucinda and I will be eating out this evening, and the three of you can order in a pizza or something. Is that okay with everyone?''

''That's fine with me,'' Nick said quickly.

Carlotta shrugged. ''It's all right by me.''

''Good morning, everyone.'' Lucinda came in wearing a bright smile. ''You were out late last night,'' she said to Nick. ''Is everything all right at Bobby's?''

''Everything's fine,'' he replied. ''It just took longer to install that software on his computer than I thought.''

''Good, good.'' Dan put his arm around Lucinda. ''I'll go wake up Chloe and then we can make our announcement.''

''Chloe's not upstairs,'' Nick said. ''We don't know where she is.''

''She went for a walk,'' Lucinda explained. ''There was a note taped to the front door. I saw it when I got the paper.''

''A walk. Chloe?'' Dan laughed and hugged Lucinda. ''Well, I guess we should wait until she gets back, but I have a feeling these two have already figured it all out.''

''You're not splitting up?'' Nick cried happily. He

was vaguely aware that this news would have been even better if Chloe had been here to share it with him.

"No, we're not," Lucinda replied. "But there will be some changes around here. For starters, I'm going back to work." She looked at Dan. "It took a lot of arguing and a lot of compromising, but we both agreed that one of the problems we've had is that I've been bored."

"Okay, okay, I'll admit my ego took a bruising at the thought of my wife working. But now I understand how important it is that you have your own thing—" He broke off as the doorbell chimed. "Who could that be?"

"Maybe it's Chloe." Nick leapt off the stool and ran for the front door. He yanked it open and then blinked in surprise. Two men stood there. One of them was middle-aged and wearing a blue blazer, white shirt, and bow tie, and the other, younger one wore jeans and a polo shirt and had a camera slung around his neck.

The older one stepped forward. "Hi, I'm Jack Lehman, a reporter from the *Landsdale News*." He smiled and handed Nick his card. "This is Hank Rickman, my photographer."

"Hi," Nick said. "Uh, what—"

"Is it Chloe?" Dan asked as he walked up behind his stepson.

"Are you Chloe Marlowe's father?" the reporter asked.

"Yes." Dan's face grew serious. "Why is the press interested in my daughter?"

"The press is always interested in heroes," Lehman said. "Or in this case, a heroine. We'd like to have a few words with her, if you don't mind."

"Heroine?" Dan shook his head in confusion and glanced at Nick before turning back to the reporters. "Why don't you come in. I'm afraid I'm a bit confused."

They stepped into the foyer.

Dan looked at Nick again. "Do you have any idea?"

Nick shook his head, but a funny feeling was creeping up his spine. A feeling he didn't like very much. "No, not a clue."

"Dan?" Lucinda said as she joined her husband. "What's going on?"

"These men are from the Landsdale newspaper," Dan explained. "They want to see Chloe. But I don't know why."

"Your daughter apparently didn't say anything about what happened yesterday, did she?" Lehman said with a grin. "Well, Chloe Marlowe, at great personal risk to herself, saved a little boy's life."

Nick went rigid as the implications of the words sank in. Chloe had saved someone's life?

"She didn't say a word," Dan yelped. "She saved some kid's life. . . ."

"At great personal risk to her own, as I said," Lehman offered. "She pulled a little kid out from in front of a speeding truck. According to the trucker, she was inches and seconds away from getting killed herself."

"That's how we found out about it," the photographer interjected. "The driver was so impressed by her bravery, he gave us a call. We've verified the story with the boy's parents. Can we see her now? We'd like to hear what she has to say and get a picture, if that's okay by you.''

Nick slowly backed away. He had to get moving; he had to find Chloe.

"I can't believe it," Dan muttered. Shocked, he was shaking his head. "My little Chloe, a heroine."

Nick made it to the kitchen. "Do you have any idea where Chloe could have gone?" he asked Carlotta.

"None. What's goin' on?"

"There's some reporters out there," he explained as he headed for the back door. "They say Chloe saved a kid's life yesterday."

"My God, really?" Carlotta beamed with pride. "That girl really *has* changed."

"I know, I know. That's why I've got to find her." Nick yanked open the door. "Are you sure you don't know where she's gone?"

Carlotta's smile vanished as she realized that Nick was seriously worried. "I don't know what's going on and maybe one of these days you'll see fit to tell me. Chloe's acted funny ever since that accident. If I was you, I'd start there."

As Nick hadn't any other ideas, he decided it was as good a place as any to go.

Chloe's feet hurt by the time she reached her destination. She stood for a moment and stared at the huge tree she'd plowed her car into less than two weeks ago. There were two huge horizontal gashes on the bark, but other than that, the tree had come out of the accident a lot better than her car. She wandered over and ran her hand along the rough surface. Her life had changed so completely in the split second she'd lost control of the car. Had she been speeding? She couldn't really remember. At first, she'd been certain the accident had been her fault. But now she wasn't so sure. Now she wondered if maybe fate or destiny or whatever had ordained that she smash into this poor tree so that she could die.

And then change.

Chloe sat down, crossed her legs, and got comfortable. She wasn't expecting any great revelations. It wasn't as if the tree were going to talk or tell her any secrets of the universe. But this place gave her a measure of peace. She didn't know why. Didn't care, either. She just needed a place to think about what had happened yesterday.

About that split second when she'd hesitated to run toward that speeding truck.

She'd been scared. She hadn't wanted to die.

Chloe idly reached over and picked up a strand of long, dried grass. She started peeling off the outer layers. It hadn't been the fear of death that had made her hesitate. It had been that life was so sweet. Death didn't frighten her; having been there, so to speak, she'd never be frightened again. She'd hesitated because she'd realized she wasn't ready to give this up yet. And that's what made her feel so lousy. She'd hesitated when it came to doing what she'd been sent back to do.

Now she felt guilty.

She'd completed her mission. Her time was probably going to be up soon.

That's why she felt so guilty. She wasn't ready to go back to the light. Not yet. There were too many things she wanted to do. So much to learn and experience. Too many places to go and people to love.

She wanted to see an igloo and ride an outrigger canoe. She wanted to study French and climb a pyramid. The world was so huge and beautiful. She wanted to take up hiking and white-water rafting, see the stars from the floor of the desert, and feel the wind against her face before a rainstorm.

Since she'd died, she'd come to realize how very sweet life was. And she wasn't ready to let it go. Oh blast, she thought, maybe I'm just a coward after all.

The sound of screaming brakes jerked her out of her reverie. She looked over her shoulder just as Nick's Chevy screeched to a halt behind her. Chloe jumped to her feet. "What's wrong?" she cried. "Is it Dad?"

"Nothing's wrong except you scaring the hell out of me," Nick yelled. "Why didn't you tell us?"

"All I did was go for a walk," she said. But she had a good idea he wasn't just referring to her morning hike.

Nick stopped in front of her and put his hands on his hips. "You know good and well what I mean. Why didn't you tell us about saving that kid?"

"Oh, that."

"Yeah, that. Jeez, Chloe. I almost had a stroke when those reporters showed up."

"Reporters? What reporters?"

"From the local paper," Nick explained. Now that he saw she was okay, he felt much better. Not 100 percent yet—that wouldn't come until they straightened out some of her crazy ideas—but he felt good that she was all right. "They're at the house now giving your dad an earful."

"How did they find out? . . ." She shook her head in confusion.

"The trucker was so impressed with your Wonder Woman act he gave them a call." Nick sank down on the ground, and Chloe sat down next to him.

Neither of them said anything for a moment. Then Nick broke the silence. "You should have told me, Chloe. I thought we were sort of close now."

"I was going to tell you," she said, "but you got home so late last night and then I left so early this morning. . . ."

"Why'd you leave?" Nick pressed. "Why'd you come here?"

Chloe shrugged and looked away. "I guess because this is where it all started. This is where I died. Well, not here exactly; I mean, I was in the ambulance and all. But I don't exactly know the spot where I pegged out. . . ."

"You think you've done what you were sent back to do, don't you?" he blurted. Until they confronted that problem, until he got her to admit she couldn't be sure, he wasn't going to feel relieved.

She nodded.

"You think you're going to die now, don't you?" he said softly.

Again, she nodded.

"You're wrong, Chloe." He reached up and gently grabbed her chin, turned her to face him. "You can't possibly know when your time is up. None of us can know that."

"I'm different," she said, "I can—"

"Of course you're different," he interrupted. "None of us are anything like anyone else. That's what makes being human such a gas. I know what you're going to say. I know you died and went down the tunnel, et cetera, et cetera, et cetera. But I've done some reading on the subject too. . . ."

"You have?"

"Yeah, and your experience isn't unique."

"I never said it was," she protested.

"Don't get all huffy on me," he soothed. "My point is, lots of people have done the tunnel thing and come back with a sense of purpose. Some of them even report that they feel they've achieved their purpose and then go on to live a long, happy life. You can too."

Chloe wanted to believe him. She wanted to believe that it wasn't going to end soon. That she still had time to do some of the things she wanted. That there was still time to contribute her bit of good to the world. "Do you really think so?"

"Of course I do," he said earnestly. "Like I said, I've done a lot of research on the subject. As a matter of fact, that's why I was so late getting home last night. I was on the Internet about this."

Chloe felt her spirits lift. Maybe Nick was right. She glanced down at the scraped knees and laughed.

"Well, I did save the kid yesterday and I'm not dead yet."

"You're not going to die," he insisted. "And it really bugs me that you keep talking yourself into an early grave. Knock it off."

She regarded him thoughtfully. "Why does it bother you so much?"

Now it was his turn to look away.

"Well?" she persisted. She punched him lightly on the arm. "Tell me. You come unglued every time I talk about my death or dying . . . or—"

"Because I like you, you dummy," he snapped. "I always have. Even when you were a spoiled brat. No one likes to hear someone they care about being so damned casual about death."

"You like me?" Chloe's spirits soared. "Really? You mean it?" She'd hoped his asking her for a date wasn't just a reaction to their working together to reconcile their folks. "Even when I was a spoiled, self-centered little witch?"

"Don't let it go to your head," he mumbled. Then he laughed. "Yeah, I've liked you for a long time. I guess I must be a pretty smart guy. Even with all that selfish crap of yours I always knew there was a good person underneath."

She snorted in disbelief. "Please. I had to crawl on my belly like a reptile to get you to help me. . . ." She broke off and winced. "Speaking of which, I'm afraid our parents might be beyond the point of no return."

"I don't think so—" he began.

But she cut him off. "You weren't there yesterday.

They had a real knock-down-drag-out fight and then they spent the rest of the evening closeted in the bedroom. It doesn't look good. I don't suppose you've managed to actually get hold of Tina or Jason, have you?''

''I talked to them last night from Uncle Bobby's.'' Nick grinned hugely. ''They've got the rent money. They only went to Vegas because Jason got a part in a movie that was filming out in the desert. He replaced an actor who got sick. Anyway, they're staying on at the condo and sending us back the money we lent them next week. Jason's movie gig put them back in the chips.''

''That's great,'' she cried. ''That means that your mom will have to stay with Dad. . . .'' She broke off as she saw Nick shaking his head.

''Afraid not. Mom's got a job too. She made the announcement this morning.''

''Well, hell.'' Chloe got to her feet and started pacing in front of the tree. ''So we're right back where we started. But I thought you said she didn't have any money saved. That she couldn't afford to move out until she had a couple of paychecks under her belt.''

''She's not moving out.'' He leaned back on one elbow. He was enjoying this. ''As a matter of fact, she and your father made the big announcement this morning.''

''What announcement?'' Chloe asked hopefully. ''Come on, tell me. What's going on?''

Nick gave her a cocky grin. ''The divorce is off. They talked themselves blue in the face last night and came to the same conclusion we'd come to: They'd be miserable apart. They still love each other. Too bad you weren't home this morning—you could have heard the big news yourself.''

''Why, you creep,'' she began. She launched herself at him and began punching him lightly on the arms. ''Why didn't you tell me? I've been worrying myself silly.''

''I'm sorry.'' Nick grabbed at her hands and held them tightly against his chest. ''I couldn't help myself. I guess I wanted to get back at you a little for scaring me. When I realized that you'd saved that boy's life and then you were gone and everything, it put the fear of God in me.''

''Why were you scared? You didn't think I'd do something dumb, did you?'' They both knew what she was referring to. ''Just because I might have thought my time was up, that doesn't mean I'd do anything to shorten it. I've still got a lot of things to make up for.''

''I never thought that,'' he said. ''But I was scared. Sometimes you can be scared and not know exactly why.'' Still holding her hands, he got up and pulled her to her feet.

They stood under the spreading branches of the tree staring into one another's eyes. Nick lowered his head and softly, gently kissed her on the mouth.

Chloe kissed him back. She wasn't sure what was going to happen between them. But she'd learned one of the great secrets of life: No one knew what was going to happen tomorrow or the next day or the next. You had to live every day like it was your last. No one was promised a tomorrow.

Nick drew back and smiled at her. "What do you think our parents are going to think of this?" he asked teasingly.

"You mean you and me?"

"Yeah."

Chloe laughed. "My dad will have a cow and your mom will calm him down. Then he'll realize you're a pretty cool guy and I could do a lot worse."

"You ready to go back now and face everyone?"

She took a deep breath. "You think that reporter will still be there?"

"Probably." Nick shrugged. "We haven't been gone that long. Why? Do you want to avoid talking to him?"

"Well, I don't want to be made out to be a big heroine or anything," she admitted. "It was no big deal."

"Chloe, you saved the boy's life." He pulled her toward the car. "Take it from me, it was a big deal. Just ask his parents. And I think people *ought* to make a fuss over you. What you did was heroic. The world needs heroes, Chloe."

"Okay, if you say so," she said doubtfully, "I'll do it. But I tell you, I don't feel like a hero at all. I just feel like a person. A *good* one, finally."

"Come on, Chloe. Let's go home."